"What do you want?"

Lacey recognized the tightness that surrounded her heart. "After all," she continued, "we both know that it can't possibly be me."

She heard Lewis make a small sound. It could have been one of shock, it could have been disgust. She wanted to turn around and confront him to tell him that there could be no purpose in his being here in her hallway, but she lacked the courage to do so, knew that if she turned and looked at him now . . .

"I came to talk to you about Jessica."

He knew. He must know. He had guessed . . . or worked out . . . but how could he know?

"Tell me, Lacey. *Is* she my child? I *have* to know."

PENNY JORDAN was constantly in trouble in school because of her inability to stop daydreaming—especially during French lessons. In her teens, she was an avid romance reader, although it didn't occur to her to try writing one herself until she was older. "My first half-dozen attempts ended up ingloriously," she remembers, "but I persevered, and one manuscript was finished." She plucked up the courage to send it to a publisher, convinced her book would be rejected. It wasn't, and the rest is history! Penny is married and lives in Cheshire, England.

Penny Jordan's striking mainstream novel *Power Play* quickly became a *New York Times* bestseller. She followed that success with *Silver*, a story of ambition, passion and intrigue and *The Hidden Years*, a novel that lays bare the choices all women face in their search for love.

Watch for Penny's latest blockbuster, *Lingering Shadows*, available in August.

Books by Penny Jordan

HARLEQUIN PRESENTS
1476—SECOND TIME LOVING
1491—PAYMENT DUE
1508—A FORBIDDEN LOVING
1529—A TIME TO DREAM
1544—DANGEROUS INTERLOPER
1552—SECOND-BEST HUSBAND

PENNY JORDAN

A CURE FOR LOVE

Harlequin Books

TORONTO • NEW YORK • LONDON
AMSTERDAM • PARIS • SYDNEY • HAMBURG
STOCKHOLM • ATHENS • TOKYO • MILAN
MADRID • WARSAW • BUDAPEST • AUCKLAND

Harlequin Presents first edition August 1993
ISBN 0-373-11575-X

Original hardcover edition published in 1991
by Mills & Boon Limited

A CURE FOR LOVE

CHAPTER ONE

'ARE you ready yet, Mum? Honestly, I feel as nervous as though I were the one having to make the speech.'

'I'm not making a speech, merely handing over the cheque to Dr Hanson,' Lacey Robinson responded to her daughter's excited chatter.

In point of fact she was guilty of evasion. She *was* nervous. Helping to raise the money for the research into the rare and devastating disease—which, while carried in the female genes only, manifested itself in physical symptoms in the male sex, like haemophilia and other similar disorders—had been one thing. Standing up in public to hand over to the hospital the cheque for the money they had raised was another.

She had already told herself very firmly that such self-consciousness was ridiculous in a woman of thirty-eight with a nineteen-year-old daughter, but that hadn't stopped the butterflies at present crowding her stomach.

'I'm so proud of you, Ma,' Jessica told her, crossing the kitchen to come and put her arms round her and give her a hug. Of the two of them Jessica was easily the taller, topping her mother's slender five-foot-two frame by a good four inches, but their colouring was the same. Both of them had the same silky fine dark hair and the same wide-spaced grey eyes, the same unexpectedly full lips, although in Lacey's case there was a vulnerability about her features which was missing from those of her more ebullient daughter.

'*I* haven't done anything,' Lacey protested now. 'It's the people who donated the money in response to our appeal who deserve recognition and praise.'

'Yes, of course,' Jessica agreed. 'But *you* were the one who organised everything, who first started the appeal.'

'Only after I'd heard about little Michael Sullivan at work. It was so heartbreaking. I still don't know how on earth Declan and Cath have managed to come to terms with the tragedy of it. To have lost two children before little Michael, from the same inherited disorder...'

'Can Michael ever be cured?' Jessica asked her quietly.

'No, not cured, but with the money we've raised further research can take place into ways of alleviating the effect of the deterioration of the central motor system, and of course, now that they've managed to isolate the gene which causes the disease, a... Well, with the new techniques they have for discovering the sex of an embryo at a very early stage in a pregnancy, the parents can opt to have only girls who, while they carry the disease, are not affected by it.'

'You mean that now the Sullivans could choose to have only daughters?'

'Yes.'

'Well, I don't care what you say, I'm still proud of you,' Jessica told her warmly, adding, 'I'm glad they decided to have the presentation now, while I'm at home.'

Jessica was in her first year at Oxford, taking a degree course which would one day equip her with excellent qualifications. If Jessica was proud of her, then how much more was she proud of her daughter? Lacey reflected lovingly.

Life had not been easy for Jessica, an only child, a fatherless child... A child without the financial advantages of many of her peers, she could so easily have grown up rebellious and resentful, unhappy and alone, but, almost right from the moment she was born, she had been a sunny-natured, happy child.

It was typical of Lacey that she herself took no credit for her daughter and, as she wryly told friends, she could certainly take no credit for her scholastic abilities, nor her excellence at sports. Those were qualities—gifts—Jessica had received from her father.

'Come back, Ma. Where are you?' Jessica teased her now, waving her hand in front of Lacey's face and grinning at her.

'You know what I think, don't you?' Jessica commented thoughtfully ten minutes later when they were both in Lacey's small car, driving towards the civic hall where the presentation was to take place. 'I think that our Dr Hanson rather fancies you, Ma.'

Lacey flushed. She couldn't help it. That was the curse of her pale Celtic skin colouring.

Jessica saw this betraying reaction and laughed before asking semi-seriously, 'Why have you never remarried, Ma? I mean, I know you loved him, but after he'd left you, when it was all over and you were divorced...didn't you ever...haven't there...?'

'Been other men?' Lacey invited wryly.

It was her policy and always had been to be as open and as honest with her daughter as she could, and, although this wasn't a topic they had ever discussed before, she sensed that, now that Jessica was living away from home, she was beginning to look far more questioningly at her mother's past, at her life, comparing it perhaps to the lives of other women of the same age.

'Well at first I was too... too upset ... too...'

'Devastated,' Jessica supplied for her. 'I know he was my father, but how he could have done that to you ...?'

'It wasn't really his fault, Jess. He fell out of love with me. It happens.'

'And you were never tempted to tell him about me. I mean ...'

'Yes ... yes, I was tempted,' Lacey admitted honestly. 'But he'd already made it clear to me that he didn't love me any longer; that he wanted our marriage to end. I didn't know until after he'd left that I was expecting you; perhaps I should have.'

'No... no, Ma. You did the right thing ... the only thing,' Jessica assured her quickly, putting her hand over her mother's and giving her a warm smile. 'Don't you ever think you didn't. I know people whose parents stuck it out supposedly for their sakes. It must be awful to be brought up in that kind of atmosphere, never really knowing if both your parents are going to be there when you get home from school, feeling they're only to-gether because of you. No, I might only have had you but I've never, never doubted that you loved me and wanted me.'

For a moment the two women exchanged looks of shared love and respect and then Jessica reminded her mother slyly, 'But you still haven't answered my original question.'

'No. Well, as I said at first, it was the last thing on my mind, and then as you grew older ... Well, to be honest with you, Jess, there just never seemed to be the time, or at least it's probably more honest to say that there never was a man for whom I wanted to make the time.'

'Perhaps you were afraid ... afraid of allowing anyone to get too close to you in case they hurt you the way he ... the way my father hurt you,' Jessica suggested shrewdly.

'Perhaps,' Lacey agreed.

'Well, it can't have been because you didn't have the opportunity,' Jessica added forthrightly.

She laughed when Lacey flushed again.

'Oh, Ma ... sometimes you make me feel as though *you're* the little girl. Look at you! I've seen the way men give you a second look, the way they watch you. And it's not just because you look sexy.'

When Lacey started to object, she overruled her and went on firmly.

'No, I don't care how much you try to deny it, you are; but it's not just that ... it's something else. Something to do with the fact that you're so small and ... and vulnerable-looking.'

'Well I may be short on inches, but that does *not* make me vulnerable,' Lacey told her quickly.

It was a sensitive issue, this obvious vulnerability she knew she possessed and yet seemed unable to do anything about. Others had commented on it, women friends . . . men. She knew that it was, like Jessica herself, something that had come with her marriage, or rather with the ending of it. But the last thing she wanted to do this evening was to think about the past.

Even now there were still times when she dreamed about it . . . about him . . . and in those dreams still remembered. When she woke up her response to the remembered hand against her skin was so acute, so sharp that the realisation that it was just a dream seemed impossible to accept. And there were other dreams . . . dreams when she cried out her shock, her disbelief, her anguish, and woke up with her face wet with tears.

Oddly enough those dreams had intensified since Jessica had gone to university. It was almost as though her subconscious self had tried to restrain them while Jessica was there, knowing how much she would hate her daughter to be upset . . . to know how very intensely she still remembered events which were over months before her daughter's birth.

At first she had put it down to the fact that she was missing Jess . . . the fact that she was, for the first time in twenty years, really alone; and yet her life was busy and fulfilled. She had a good job ... good friends ... and, since she had got herself involved in the fund-raising for little Michael, she scarcely seemed to have had a moment to call her own.

Tonight was the culmination of many months of hard work, bringing Michael's plight to the attention of the country via the media, raising money through all manner of events for research into ways of alleviating the distressing physical and mental deterioration suffered by children like Michael, children who rarely survived to adulthood—although there were varying degrees of severity and admittedly there had been very rare instances in which male children born to female carriers of the gene seemed to have escaped unscathed but these instances were far too rare to form the basis for any kind of detailed research.

Their small country town was lucky in having a very good local hospital, and now, with the money they had raised, further research could be done. It couldn't bring back the two sons the Sullivans had already lost, of course, Lacey acknowledged sadly as she parked her car outside the civic hall.

They were halfway across the car park when Jessica, who had been walking a couple of yards behind her, suddenly caught up with her, taking hold of her arm and giving her a small shake as she told her with a soft laugh, 'There—see—it's happened again: A man just getting out of the smoothest-looking car you've ever seen was really giving you the eye.'

'Jessica!' Lacey protested. 'Honestly. I——'

'OK, OK, but it seems so wrong that you should be on your own like this, Mum. You're only thirty-eight. You should marry again... I *hate* the thought of you spending the rest of your life on your own. One of our tutors was saying the other day that there are women now, career women, who are marrying for the first time in their late thirties and having children... that the mature older woman with young children will soon be more the norm... that people *won't* feel so isolated when they get older because they will still have children at home... and——'

'Ah, I see where this is all leading: you're worried that I'm going to become a burden to you in my old age. Well, I've got news for you, my darling daughter: I don't *need* a husband to produce children.'

'No, but you *do* need a man,' Jessica told her bluntly. 'And it isn't that. You know that. It's just that I'm beginning to realise how much you missed out on, and if you want the truth I feel guilty, Ma. If it hadn't been for me, you could——'

'Stop right there,' Lacey told her firmly. 'If it hadn't been for you I'd probably have given up and... and done something very, very silly indeed,' she said quietly and truthfully, watching the shock register in her daughter's eyes. 'You were my lifeline, Jess. You were my reason for going on living. Without you——'

'You really loved him that much?' Jessica shivered. 'Oh, God, Ma, I'm never, ever going to let myself be vulnerable to a man like that.'

Lacey felt her heart sink. She had been afraid of this. Afraid that in her honesty she might have warped Jessica's own attitude to love.

'Loving someone always makes you vulnerable, Jess, but that doesn't mean it's bad.' She pushed Jessica's long hair off her face and smiled at her. 'You *will* fall in love, you know,' she told her softly. 'And, when you do, you'll wonder how you can ever have believed you wouldn't, I promise you.'

She prayed that she was right, and that Jessica wouldn't cut herself off from the happiness that loving someone would bring her just because of her experience.

After all, it was quite true. Lacey *could* have gone on to form another relationship, to have married a second time. The fact that she had chosen not to was... Well, as she had already told Jessica, there had simply never been a man who had made her feel that she wanted to.

Or was it that she had never *allowed* there to be a man who might have made her feel that way?

Uncomfortably she pushed away the thought. What was the matter with her? She had far more important things on her mind right now than dwelling on the past; on something she should have overcome years ago. It was twenty years since her marriage had broken up, for heaven's sake. Twenty years. A lifetime, and yet sometimes...sometimes she would see a man in the distance, and something about the way he moved, the turn of his head...would set her heart racing, her stomach cramping, and it would all come sweeping over her again. The elation, the desolation, the joy...the grief...the pain, the anguish...the disbelief and the anger.

She hadn't realised she had stopped walking until Jessica caught hold of her arm and said teasingly, 'It's no use, Ma. Too late to back out now. They're all waiting for you in there.' She eyed Lacey's elegant navy dress with its white collar critically and added, 'I still think the walking shorts and that snazzy little jacket with the gold stripes would have looked terrific on you...'

Recalling the eye-catching outfit Jessica was describing, Lacey grinned at her and retorted, 'For someone your age with endless legs maybe; for me—never!'

The civic hall was packed, the sea of faces confronting her as people turned their heads to register her entrance, panicking her for a moment, even though she had thought she was prepared.

She had never liked crowds, preferring solitude, anonymity—a legacy from her childhood at the children's home where she had grown up after the death of her parents—and she suspected that without Jessica standing behind her and blocking her exit she might almost have been tempted to turn, run and disappear.

Thank goodness for Jess. How humiliating it would have been if she were to give way to that silly juvenile impulse...and now Ian Hanson was coming towards her, smiling at her...

As Jessica had so sapiently remarked, had Lacey indicated that she would welcome it he would probably have been keen to take their relationship to a more personal level.

As it was she liked him, just as she liked her boss, Tony Aimes, but for neither of them did she feel the emotional, or sexual, desire that might have encouraged her to respond to their overtures. Both of them were divorced, both of them had children, both of them were kind, attractive men, but, much as she liked them as people, as men they left her completely cold, completely untouched...unaroused.

Because she *deliberately* chose to stay that way? Because she was afraid? Angry with her train of thought, she tried to remind herself why she was here. Tonight was most certainly not the night for that kind of immature and self-centred soul-searching.

Tonight was Michael's night; Michael's and the night of all those who had given so generously to their cause.

She had been very apprehensive at first when she had been nominated by the other members of their fund-raising committee to be the one to publicly hand over the cheque to the hospital, but rather than cause a fuss she had unwillingly agreed to do so.

Tony Aimes had suggested that after the presentation they might go out together somewhere for a celebratory meal, but she had gently refused, just as she had refused a similar invitation from Ian Hanson, explaining truthfully that, since she saw so little of Jessica now that her daughter was at Oxford, she intended to spend the evening with her.

The trouble was that, while she liked both men as friends, and while the last thing she wanted to do was to hurt anyone's feelings, she knew enough of the anguish of loving someone and then finding out that the love they professed to feel in return was only a cruel sham to ever wish to inflict that kind of pain on anyone else, so she had no wish to have a more intimate relationship with either of them.

She had known Tony Aimes for many years. She had originally moved to this part of the world following the break-up of her marriage.

Housing here had been relatively cheap then, and as Lacey had been a divorcee with a baby on the way—and very little money—that had been an important consideration.

When Jessica's father had announced that he didn't love her any more and that he wanted a divorce, he had told her that she could keep the marital home, that all he wanted was his freedom; but her pride would not allow her to do that, and so after the divorce had become final she had sold the house and scrupulously forwarded to his solicitor half the proceeds of its sale.

She had never received any acknowledgement of his receipt of the money but then she had not expected to do so. From the day he had walked into their kitchen and announced that he no longer loved her he had also walked out of her life, and her only contact with him had been via their solicitors.

People started to clap as she walked towards the small stage. She could feel the hot burn of embarrassed colour sweeping her skin. At thirty-eight she ought to be long past the stage of blushing like a schoolgirl, she told herself ruefully; long, long past it.

It seemed she was the last to arrive—the others were already up on the stage, little Michael squirming excitedly in his chair as she went to join them.

She couldn't help it; as she saw him smiling at her her eyes filled with tears, not of sadness, but of joy—joy in people's generosity and warmth, and joy in Michael's innocent love of life.

At the moment his illness was in remission; he had received a stay of execution, but for how long?

As she bent to hug and kiss him, she prayed that somehow a miracle could happen and that Michael could be saved; but there were so many other Michaels in the world, so many other children who...

She checked her thoughts, reminding herself that emotionalism did nothing to help Michael, that it wasn't sitting in a corner crying which had raised the money to further research, but other people's generosity and hard work.

As she took her place with the others she glanced down into the mass of people gathered in the hall. She could see Jessica sitting in the front row, not far from Tony Aimes.

Was it really almost twenty years ago that she had first started working for Tony as his secretary? Where on earth had the years gone?

During that time Tony had been married and then divorced; Jessica had grown from a baby to a woman; and she—what had she done with her life? What had she achieved on a personal level?

She had financial security, a very pleasant lifestyle, and she knew that many people would have envied her. There were others though, she knew, who looked at her and pitied her for her single, manless state.

That had never worried her. Better by far to live alone in contentment and peace than to suffer the kind of anguish which she knew all too well could come from loving another person. Especially when, like her, one had a propensity to love too well...too intensely, perhaps, and certainly too unwisely.

The chairman of their small committee was getting to his feet, explaining for the benefit of the audience the purpose of their fund-raising. Her stomach muscles knotted and tensed as she waited for her own cue, the moment when she would have to get up and hand over the cheque to Ian.

She had rehearsed her few lines over and over again and was surely word-perfect by now. All she really had to do was to add her thanks to those of the chairman, and then hand over the cheque to Ian.

At the back of the hall people from the local radio station and TV company were busily recording the event, and the movement of the camera, catching the light momentarily, distracted her so that she looked away from the stage and into the audience.

Quite how it happened she had no real idea; quite why she should so unerringly pick out one face among so many, and a face she had not seen in twenty years, moreover... Surely it should not have been possible for her to recognise him so instantly, to know with that gut-wrenching, heart-stopping surge of awareness that it *was* him, even from that one brief glance; but it was.

Lewis was here. Here in the civic hall... here in her home-town...here in the place, the life she had built so determinedly to exclude him... to exclude everything about him.

Everything bar the child he had given her; and the pain he had inflicted upon her.

Lewis Marsh... her husband... her lover. The only man she had *ever* loved... *ever* wanted. The man she had thought loved her in the same way... the man who had told her that he did love her, who had begged her to marry him, who had told her that they would always be together, throughout life and throughout eternity.

Eternity! Their marriage had lasted just over a year.

She started to tremble violently, her heart pounding with sick shock as her brain refused to take in what her eyes were telling her.

It must be a mistake; it couldn't possibly be Lewis.

She had, out of shock and self-protection, already focused her gaze as far away from him as she possibly could, but now, like a child anxiously searching a darkened room for an imagined monster, she looked hesitantly back, searching the packed hall feverishly, praying that she had been mistaken.

Twenty years was, after all, a long time . . . long enough for mistakes to be made, for her memory to play tricks on her. The Lewis she remembered no longer existed. Like her, he would have changed, grown older.

The sickness returned. If she had recognised him, then had he . . .? She stopped searching. Her brain was trying to perform impossible acrobatics with far too many confusing thoughts.

What if by some impossible chance it *was* Lewis? Even if he *had* recognised her he was hardly likely to walk up on to the stage and announce to the world that she had once been his wife, was he? Why was she so afraid?

She wasn't afraid, she told herself stoutly. She was just shocked...taken aback...and no doubt she had made a mistake anyway. It couldn't possibly be Lewis. Why should it be? No; her belief that she had seen him was just a by-product of her nervousness about presenting the cheque.

Presenting the cheque! She tensed, appalled to realise that she had stopped following the chairman's speech; that, in the space of half a dozen seconds or so, the purpose of her presence on the stage had been totally submerged by the shock of thinking she had seen her ex-husband, and now as she feverishly concentrated on what the chairman was saying she realised that it was almost time for her to stand up and make the presentation.

'And so now I should like to hand you over to our chief fund-raiser, without whom this whole appeal would never have been launched—Lacey Robinson.'

Lacey stood up. She had reverted to her maiden name after the divorce, and now, for some reason, as she got to her feet her glance darted almost guiltily towards the packed hall, almost as though she expected Lewis to stand up and announce that she was masquerading under a false name; and yet, even if by some extraordinary mischance it was Lewis, why on earth should he object to her reversion to her maiden name? It was *he* after all, who had brought their marriage to an end . . . who had announced that it was over, that he no longer loved her . . . that there was someone else . . .

This time as she scanned the hall there was no familiar male face, no malely autocratic profile, no sleek, well-groomed dark head—no one in fact who remotely resembled the man she had married, the man who had fathered Jessica, the man she had loved to the point where without him her life had no purpose, no reason other than that somehow she must keep on going for the sake of their child, the child he hadn't even known she had conceived; the child he had already told her he wouldn't have wanted.

'You want domesticity... children... I don't,' he had told her flatly, ignoring her feeble attempt to interrupt him, to protest that when he had told her how much he had loved her, how much he had wanted her as his wife, he had said how much he wanted her to have his children, how much he shared with her a longing for the domestic family life neither of them had ever really known—she because of her parents' death, and he through the divorce which had split up his parents while he was still very young.

Somehow or other she managed to make her short speech and hand over the cheque, although her hands were trembling violently when Ian took it from her.

Afterwards, when it was all over, Jessica came hurrying anxiously towards her, asking her if she was all right.

'You had such an odd look on your face when you were on the stage. I even thought for a moment you were just going to get up and walk out. I know you were nervous, but I hadn't realised ... Anyway, it's over now,' she comforted her.

Lacey gave a vague smile.

'Never mind, Ma, you were brill, despite your nerves,' Jessica told her, tucking her arm through her mother's. 'And now how about that meal you promised me, before one of your admirers pounces on you and persuades you to let him join us?'

Lacey gave her a wan look. In reality the last thing she felt like doing was going out to eat. Her stomach was still performing somersaults and her heart felt as though it had literally been squeezed in a vice.

She felt both sick and shaky, like someone suffering from the aftermath of a nerve-shattering shock. She told herself that she was being ridiculous; that she was a grown woman, and surely long past the stage of reacting like that simply because she thought she had seen a man whose memory she ought to have put behind her years ago.

'Quickly,' Jessica hissed. 'Tony's heading this way.' As they headed for the exit she added drily, 'Honestly, Ma, I don't know why you don't marry poor Tony. He adores you, you know, and he always has. Think of the life you'd have—he'd spoil you to death.'

'I like him, but I don't love him,' Lacey told her, surprising herself as much as her daughter, who stopped and turned to look at her. 'Is that so very shocking,' she asked Jessica defensively, 'that at my age I should consider love a prerequisite for marriage? I suppose to someone of your age it probably is.'

'No...you've got it all wrong. Of course I don't think you're too old to fall in love. I was just surprised that you should *want* to. I've always had the impression that because of what happened with...with my father that we...that you'd written sexual love out of your life so to speak. I thought that you'd actually prefer the kind of relationship you could have with Tony—him spoiling you...pampering you...'

'That wouldn't be fair to him,' Lacey told her quietly.

'No, I suppose not. But there must be times when you feel lonely...when you want——'

'Sex,' Lacey supplied bluntly for her, surprising herself a second time.

Jessica gave her a sideways look. 'Well... yes...although I wouldn't have put it quite as directly as that,' she told her a little defensively.

Lacey shook her head, and then wondered if she was being entirely honest. Weren't there times even now when she woke up tense and aching, her body reminding her that there had once been a time when she hadn't slept alone, when she had known the caresses of a lover, when she . . .

'What I want right now is my dinner,' she fibbed, completely redirecting the conversation. 'I've booked a table at that new Italian place. It's supposed to be very good.'

It was—at least to judge from the enjoyment Jessica was exhibiting. For her part, Lacey found that she just simply didn't have any appetite.

'Ma, what's wrong?' Jessica started to ask her, and then broke off to say admiringly, 'Mm . . . now that's what I call a man! Pity he's too old for me.'

Lacey turned her head in automatic response to Jessica's comment.

Three men had just walked into the restaurant, but she only saw one of them. This time there was no possibility of a mistake . . . no doubt. It was like a massive blow to the heart, numbing her body into complete immobility.

Lewis. It *was* Lewis!

'Ma, what is it . . . what's wrong? You look as though you've just seen a ghost,' Jessica told her worriedly.

A ghost. She gave a deep shudder, her mouth twisting painfully.

Behind her she could hear Lewis's voice—deep, masculine, so agonisingly familiar, so shockingly clearly remembered.

'Jess, I'm not feeling very well,' she said shakily. 'Would you mind if we left?'

The men had walked past them now, leaving Lacey free to stand up as she kept her back towards them. Small chance of Lewis's recognising *her*; why should he? she reflected with an unfamiliar stab of sharp bitterness.

She meant nothing to him. He probably didn't even remember that she had ever existed. She wondered if he was still with *her*, the woman he had left her for, or if she too had suffered her fate; if he had gone on to fall out of love with her as well.

She pushed herself free of the table, shivering sickly, glad of Jessica's warm protective arm around her shoulders as her daughter came to her side and said anxiously, 'Ma, something's wrong. Look, let's get you home, and then I'm going to call Ian Hanson.'

Behind her she was aware of movement, of someone tensing, turning, but she couldn't look back, couldn't do anything other than freeze and shiver, aching to escape, knowing it was impossible to explain to Jessica just what was wrong, hating herself for causing her daughter this anxiety and for spoiling their last evening together... but how could she turn to Jessica now and say 'You know that man you were just admiring? Well, he's your father'?

She had always been honest with Jessica about her marriage, and told her when she was in her teens that she would never stand in her way if she ever felt she wanted to contact her father, but Jessica had remained adamant that she didn't, that she wanted nothing to do with the man who had treated her mother so cruelly, even though Lacey had painstakingly explained to her that Lewis had known nothing of her pregnancy... had not realised that she was already carrying his child when he'd announced that he wanted a divorce.

'You'd better let me drive,' Jessica announced when they got to the car. 'You went so white in there. *Is* something wrong, Ma?' she asked anxiously. 'I know you and how you hate me to worry about anything.'

'Nothing's wrong,' Lacey fibbed firmly. 'I think I'm just suffering a bit of over-reaction to this evening. I was dreading giving that speech. You know what a baby I am about public events. I'm sorry I let it spoil our meal, though.'

'Well, you certainly look a lot better now. Are you sure you don't want me to call Ian?'

'Stop fussing! I'm fine. A good night's sleep and tomorrow morning I'll be back to normal.'

She knew that it wasn't true, but thankfully tomorrow morning Jessica was going back to Oxford. For the first time since her daughter had left home, Lacey actually wanted to see her go. Her mouth twisted bitterly.

CHAPTER TWO

Ten o'clock on a fine sunny morning. Lacey had the whole day ahead of her with a hundred and one things she could do, and yet all she felt like doing was crawling back to bed, like an animal seeking protection, oblivion almost, if not from life, then at least from her own thoughts... her tormenting memories.

Half an hour ago she had watched Jessica drive off, having assured her anxious daughter over and over again that she was fine.

She couldn't blame Jessica for being anxious: one look in her mirror confirmed her daughter's worried comments.

Her face looked bloodless, even with her make-up, her eyes huge and shadowed, her mouth... She shivered a little, rubbing the goose-flesh on her arms. Her mouth, always a good indicator of her feelings, looked, even to her own eyes, vulnerable, unhappy... shocked.

Dear God, if only she had been wrong. If only it hadn't been Lewis last night. She knew that she wasn't wrong. It *was* Lewis, although what he was doing here in town she had no idea—if he was still here; perhaps he had already gone. Her tension started to ease. She pictured him, driving away from the town, his wife, her successor, at his side. She pictured the back of his head, saw the speeding car, visualised its driving through the town towards the motorway network, felt her tense muscles starting to relax, told herself that she was panicking over nothing, that, horrible though the coincidence of his turning up at the restaurant had been, it meant nothing. He had obviously not recognised her. Why should he, after all? And even if he had . . .even if he had . . .

There was something wet on her face. She touched it with her hands and discovered that she was crying.

This simply would not do. She was a supposedly mature woman of thirty-eight with a daughter of nineteen to prove it; what right, what purpose did Lewis have to suddenly appear out of the blue to destroy her contentment?

Stop being so paranoid, she chided herself firmly. How could Lewis's presence in town have anything to do with her? It was pure chance, that was all; an unfortunate chance, it was true, the sight of him stirring up, as it had done, memories; images; emotions which ought to have stopped hurting her years ago.

She had, after all, only been eighteen when she'd first met him. He had been twenty-one, almost twenty-two. They had both been invited to the same birthday party, he had looked across the room, and she had known then.

What? she asked herself tiredly; that he would break her heart...destroy her life? That he would claim to love her and then turn round and tell her that love no longer existed? That their marriage was a mistake?

It was just as well that she had arranged several days' leave from work to coincide with Jessica's visit home: the last thing she felt capable of doing right now was dealing with the complexities of her job as Tony's secretary-cum-PA.

She had a meeting later on in the day at the hospital with Ian; a final sorting out of some paperwork connected with the appeal. Ian had tentatively suggested taking her out for lunch but she had gently refused.

What was wrong with her? she wondered ruefully now. Why couldn't she abandon the past, let go of her fears and inhibitions and allow herself to grow more intimately involved with another man?

She already knew the answer to that. Lewis had hurt her far too badly for her ever to want to risk suffering that kind of pain again.

Or was it more because no man whom she had met in the years since he had left her had ever come close to arousing within her the emotions which he had so easily touched than because she was afraid of allowing herself to love another man?

There was no room in her life for such immature introspection, she told herself sharply. That kind of self-indulgence was for teenagers, for young women of her daughter's age. Women of her maturity were far too sensible and far too busy to waste time dwelling on their emotions.

Or were they? Was it more that she had never allowed herself to dwell on hers because she was too frightened of what she might have to confront?

Jessica's probing questions last night about the way she lived her life, plus the shock of seeing Lewis, were having a most unwelcome effect on her—one that could surely be best banished by some hard work and a much firmer control on her treacherous thoughts.

She was meeting Ian at the hospital at two o'clock. It was eleven now and she had promised herself that this morning she would attack the greenfly on her precious roses.

Her small house did not have a large garden, but it was blessed by an enclosing brick wall, against which over the years she had lovingly trained a variety of scented old-fashioned roses.

Beneath them were borders of mixed traditional cottage garden plants—peonies, hollyhocks, delphiniums, forget-me-nots, which seeded themselves and ran half-wild, aquileas, which did the same thing, producing their pretty pink and white flowers, and catmint, which was invariably flattened by next door's fat ginger tom-cat whom she hadn't the heart to evict from his favourite patch of the scented plant.

Treating the roses for greenfly was a laborious business, especially in these ecology-conscious days, and there wasn't going to be time to complete the task before she had to leave for the hospital, which meant she would have to tackle the housework instead.

With a wistful glance at the sunny garden, she headed for the stairs to strip Jessica's bed.

The first thing she saw when she walked into the room was Jessica's old teddy bear sitting on top of the chest of drawers.

She had bought the bear for Jessica before she was born. She went over to the chest and picked up the bear, absently smoothing its worn fur, her eyes dark with shadows.

It had been a cold wet day, she remembered, her mouth twisting a little bitterly at the ease with which she recalled every detail of that particular day.

It had been the day the letter had arrived from Lewis's solicitors, setting out the formal terms of their divorce. The divorce that even then she had desperately hoped would never happen; that letter with its cold, formal prose, its heavy underlining of Lewis's desire to cut himself completely free of her. He was giving her the house, the car, the entire contents of their savings account; Lewis, unlike her, had had a moneyed background; his maternal grandparents had left him money, and it had been with this money that he had bought their pretty house and set up a business in partnership with a colleague as independent insurance brokers.

There would be money coming to her from the business . . . she need not fear she would suffer financially from the divorce—that was what he had told her that shocking day when he had walked in and told her that he wanted their marriage brought to an end.

With hindsight she recognised that there had been something wrong for some time; that he had been quiet, withdrawn from her at times; but she had assumed that it was just the pressure of setting up the new business, and she had been so young, so much still a very new wife, that she had resolutely told herself that she was being over-sensitive, that marriage could not forever be one long honeymoon, that of course there were bound to be times when all might not seem perfect; and then had come the bombshell...the discovery that Lewis didn't love her any more ... didn't want her any more ... that there was someone else and that he wanted his freedom.

She could have fought the divorce, could have made him wait out the statutory period, but her pride would never have allowed her to do that ... and as for his money...

She had allowed her solicitor to accept half the value of the house and no more, and then she had told him that she intended to move right away from the area and make a fresh start somewhere else.

It had been on her first trip here that she had bought the bear.

She had had to change trains at Birmingham. There had been a two-hour wait for her connection. She had walked out of the station into the busy, wet city streets, feeling as though her whole life had come to an end, as though there were no point in even thinking about going on.

Coming towards her down the wet road she had seen a bus, lumbering slowly closer as it picked up speed.

She could recall with complete clarity even now the sharp clearness of her brain and its processes—of assessing the speed of the bus, of knowing that all she had to do was to step out into

the street in front of it and there would be no more
pain, no more anguish, no more loneliness . . . no
more anything.

She had walked to the edge of the kerb; she had
stepped forward; she had even taken a step out
into the street, when suddenly for the first time she
had felt her baby kick.

She had covered her stomach with both hands,
an immediate, instinctively protective, wondering
gesture, shock, joy and the most bitter-sweet sharp
pain she had ever known coalescing inside her.

Someone had touched her arm then, another
woman, chiding her warningly, 'Better watch the
traffic duck. These bus drivers . . .'

And the moment of crisis was over; she was
safely back on the pavement, shaking, feeling sick,
tears pricking her eyes, but alive . . . and, more
important, her baby was alive as well.

It had been then that she had bought the bear.

She realised suddenly that its worn fur was
damp, coming abruptly out of the past to the angry realisation that she was crying again.

Mid-life blues, she taunted herself, ignoring the
evidence of Jessica's full-length mirror which denied that her still very youthful and slender figure
showed any signs of becoming middle-aged.

She had come up here to strip the bed, not to
dwell with maudlin self-pity on the past, she

reminded herself as she pulled back the duvet and very firmly put the bear back where he belonged.

At one o'clock she started to get ready for her meeting with Ian, dressing carefully in a plain navy dress enlivened with a pretty white shawl-collar, and pair of plain, elegant navy blue pumps.

It was all very well for Jessica to complain that her mother's wardrobe needed jazzing up and that she was far too young and pretty to wear such consistently dull colours: she liked classic clothes made in classic styles.

A final check of her make-up confirmed that the elegant and discreet toffees and peaches of her eyeshadow added just the right degree of emphasis to her eyes; her mouth as always caused her to pause and wince a little. Not even the most discreet and pale lipstick could disguise its fullness . . . its——

'You really have the most wonderful mouth. Just made for kissing. Just made for this . . .'

She swallowed hard. Lewis had said those words to her the night he'd proposed, whispering the compliments in between light decorous kisses which had very quickly become less light and far from decorous. She shuddered deeply, only just managing to restrain herself from actually touching her mouth, the taste of him, the memory of him so very, very sharp and clear. She had been almost totally sexually inexperienced when she and Lewis had met.

He had been her first lover...her only lover, she reminded herself drily. The general mood of the sixties seemed to have passed her by. She had certainly never experienced the urge of those of her peers who had thrown themselves into sampling all the pleasures of the so-called sexual revolution, but then more recently in conversations with her women friends she had learned that the majority of them had also married their first lover, giving rise, in some cases, to the good-humoured complaint that there had been times—especially when their families were young and their husbands busy—when they had wondered if they had somehow missed out on life.

A different, more health-conscious approach to life had brought a different set of attitudes and values, and, as Jessica had already told her with the seriousness and confidence of extreme youth, when she eventually made love it would only be with someone whose sexual history allowed her to feel safe with him.

Jessica was one of a new breed of young women who considered a career and financial independence to be the main goals of their life: marriage and a family were things that could be put on hold until these goals were achieved. Certainly with the soaring divorce rate it seemed a sensible plan. But love...emotions—could these really be summoned at will when one had decided that the time was right to admit them into one's life? Lacey was not so sure. Or was it simply that she lacked willpower...that there was something missing in her make-up that had made it impossible for her to ever really forget Lewis...to ever really forget the pain he had caused her?

It might have helped her had she been able to hate him, to direct the corrosive power of bitterness and hatred into destroying her love, but that weapon had been denied her and the terrible anguish of all her pain had been turned against herself rather than against him.

With time she had learned to tell herself that it was not her fault that he had ceased to love her; that it was not through some lack in her that he had turned to another woman; that these things happened; that they were an everyday occurrence and not something that marked her out as a pariah, a leper, a person who had failed at one of life's most important relationships. So Lewis had stopped loving her and she had been hurt...very badly hurt. Life had to go on, and somehow she had made it go on, but the scars were still there. Her fault, not his, as she had told herself over and over again down the years. Perhaps it was because she had been so young, so alone, so idealistic, so dependent almost on his love and approval that she had suffered so desperately when they were removed. Had she had more self-worth, more sense of her own special individuality, more awareness and self-respect, things might have been different, *she* might have been different. Looking back, she saw herself as weak and destructive as a clinging vine, looking to Lewis to provide every motivation within her life, slowly choking him with the intensity of her love. Was it really any wonder that he had turned away from her?

She had been determined not to swamp her daughter in the same way, scrupulously ensuring that Jessica grew up without the hindrance of a clinging, obsessive mother. No matter how much it had hurt her at times, she had always actively encouraged her daughter to be independent, to be her own person. She valued the love that existed between them, but she did not delude herself. Jessica was slowly growing away from her, slowly beginning to take her own place in the adult world.

Perhaps Jessica was right...perhaps it *was* time for her to think about her own future.

And to do what? To marry someone like Tony or Ian...a man she might like but whom she could never love, simply to avoid the loneliness of old age? Wasn't that just as pathetic and selfish as her absorbed, intensive love for Lewis? No, she was better on her own. Safer.

She checked, uncomfortable with the word which had slipped so betrayingly into her mind. What need had she for safety these days? The pain of the past was a long time behind her now. She wasn't that same girl any more. She was a woman now...a woman who was firmly in control of her own life, her own destiny. So what if Lewis had by some unfortunate coincidence appeared in her part of the world? He obviously hadn't recognised her; there was very little chance of her running into him a second time.

Perhaps not, but she knew it was that brief, shocking sight of him which was responsible for today's introspective mood, for the shadows that showed in her eyes and skin, for the pain that lurked within her, waiting for her to relax her guard.

She gave a tiny shiver as she let herself out of the house. She had things to do, a life to live, and she had promised little Michael that she would call round to see him later on this afternoon.

If she had one secret regret it was that she had not had more children. There was something so special, so magical and humbling about the knowledge that the physical expression of one's love had led to the creation of a child . . .

She got into her car and started the engine. It was high time she put those kinds of thoughts very firmly behind her, and yet, as Jessica had reminded her, at thirty-eight she was still young enough to have another child.

Another child ... Her hands gripped the steering-wheel. First she would have to find herself a lover ... a lover, not a potential father for her unborn child. A lover—the very last thing she wanted or needed in her life. What on earth was the matter with her? Was it just her conversation with Jessica which was having such an unsettling effect on her, or was it something more than that ... something to do with that disturbing sighting of Lewis ... with her dreams ... the emotions ... the needs that continued to haunt her, no matter how much she tried to deny them?

She knew it was only because Lewis had been her only lover that those embarrassing and erotic dreams that sometimes tormented her sleep should always portray him as her partner, and that in all reality their lovemaking had probably never really been quite as intense, as passionate, as fulfilling as her dreams suggested, and yet she also knew that it was those same dreams that strengthened her unwillingness to allow another man into her life; that it was those dreams, those memories that prevented her from allowing herself to find a quieter, gentler, safer happiness with another man.

It was only when she reached the roundabout close to the hospital that she recognised with a guilty start that she had driven right across town so wrapped up in her thoughts that she wasn't really aware of having done so.

It was exactly two o'clock as she walked into the hospital and told the smiling receptionist that she had an appointment with Dr Hanson.

'Yes, of course, Mrs Robinson. I'll just let him know that you're here.'

Over the years Lacey had grown accustomed to people mistakenly addressing her as Mrs Robinson. Her reversion to her maiden name had been an instinctive gesture of revulsion against retaining anything given to her by Lewis, and, although at first she had been quick to correct people and tell them that it was Miss Robinson, these days she had ceased to bother. Correction tended to disconcert or confuse them more than their mistake concerned her.

She turned away while the girl used the intercom, and then turned back to the desk when she heard her saying, 'If you'd just like to go down to Dr Hanson's office . . .'

Having thanked her and confirmed that she knew the way, Lacey set off down the corridor.

She had to pass the maternity ward on the way to Ian's office, and through the open doors she heard the mewling cry of the new born. Her insides clenched on that familiar, never forgotten mixture of anxiety and love. It didn't seem possible that it was over nineteen years since Jessica's birth. She remembered how thrilled she had been when they had told her that she had a daughter, how proud...how...how elated almost, and then later had come the panic, the depression, the tears, and the miserable desolation of knowing that she was alone in her joy, that for her there was no partner to share in the happiness of their child's birth.

The nurses had been wonderful, and luckily she had overcome her depression.

She realised that she had stopped outside the ward. Sighing to herself, she shook her head and forced herself to continue down the corridor.

The door to Ian's office was closed. She knocked briefly on it out of politeness and then opened it and walked in.

She had expected to find Ian on his own, but it wasn't the shock of realisation that someone else was with him that stopped her in her tracks; it was the discovery that the other man in his office was none other than Lewis.

Lewis... here in Ian's office. Her whole body felt heavy and cumbersome, unable to respond to the sluggish commands of her brain, and yet at the same time her stomach was churning, her metabolism racing so frantically out of control that she was afraid she might literally be sick where she stood.

Ian, apparently oblivious to her shocked distress, was smiling at her, coming over to stand beside her and put a friendly arm around her shoulders as he said warmly, 'Lewis, I'd like you to meet a very good friend of mine: Lacey Robinson. Lacey has been the main motivator behind the appeal. She's worked far harder than the rest of us put together.'

Ian gave her a fond smile.

'Did Jessica get off all right this morning? A pity that she couldn't stay on a bit longer. Still, it's her first year and she won't want to miss out on any of her tutorials. Jessica is Lacey's daughter,' Lacey heard him explaining to Lewis. 'I must admit I still find it hart to believe that Lacey is the mother of a university student.'

Lacey could feel her face beginning to burn with a mixture of shock and anxiety. She couldn't bring herself to look at her ex-husband . . . couldn't endure the contempt and disinterest she knew would be in his eyes. She knew that Ian was only meaning to flatter her, that he genuinely did believe she looked much younger than her thirty-eight years; that he genuinely did find it difficult to believe that she was Jessica's mother; but that didn't stop her from feeling hideously embarrassed as though she were one of those women who made a point of telling everyone within earshot that she had been a child bride, and that they and their daughters were more like sisters really. That kind of thing had always made her squirm and feel acutely sorry for the poor unfortunate daughters, who in some way were almost never allowed to grow up to maturity, who always seemed to be held back by their mothers' determinedly clutching on to 'youth', who were never quite as pretty or as popular as their mothers had been at their age—and yet stubbornly she refused to open her mouth and make any disclaimer. After all, why should she feel any need to justify herself in any way to Lewis?

She could see him just within the periphery of her vision. He was standing in the shadows of the room, his head slightly averted, as though he didn't want to look at her, to acknowledge her.

His hair, she realised, was still as dark as it had always been, untouched by grey and apparently as thick and vibrant as ever. She remembered how she had loved to touch it, to feel the soft springiness of its curl beneath her fingertips, envying him that natural characteristic which had been denied her. And yet he, it seemed, had been equally fascinated by the soft sleek fall of her own straight locks, praising their silkiness, saying her hair was fluid and warm like sun-stroked water. When they made love he had liked the sensation of her hair against his skin...against his body. He had coaxed her to rub herself against him like a small sleek cat, and the sound he had made in his throat when she did so had not been unlike the rusty purr of some jungle animal.

He had taught her so many things about both his sexuality and her own; not just in terms of the physical act of union, but also of the wide variety of small intimate pleasures that could arise from the lightest, most delicate, and sometimes often unexpected kind of touch. He had been both gentle and passionate, demanding and patient. He had been the best of lovers, and the worst of husbands.

She started to shiver suddenly as her body caved in under the pressure of her shock. Lewis still hadn't looked at her properly nor she at him and yet she had recalled faultlessly and unwantedly the sensation of his hands against her skin, coaxing, stroking, loving...hands which she now saw were bunched into hard, tense fists.

He moved abruptly, flexing his fingers, a gesture unfamiliar to her and which, being unfamiliar, should have released her from her bondage to her unwanted memories; but instead it eroded her self-discipline, and anguish and desolation rose up inside her. She had changed and so of course must he, and it was foolish beyond all measure of her to mourn her own lack of knowledge of something so slight as an added mannerism.

He was tense; that involuntary flexing of his fingers proved that. He had been tense the night he'd told her he didn't want her or their marriage any more, but tense in a different way: then he had used his tension as a barrier between them ... a barrier which had told her, 'Don't come any nearer. Don't even think about trying to touch me,' and yet she had done so ... foolishly, and his recoil from her had been instant and shocking, betraying his physical revulsion for her.

Alongside her, Ian was still talking.

'Lacey almost single-handedly organised the appeal for Michael Sullivan; that was why I wanted the two of you to meet. Lacey, Lewis is——'

She couldn't endure any more. The initial shock had faded now, but what was left in its place was even worse: a kind of sick anxiety, coupled with pain and something more ... something she could not bear to analyse.

'Ian, I'm sorry,' she interrupted shakily. 'I'm afraid I can't stay...'

As her dazed brain sought frantically for some excuse for her unscheduled departure, she saw out of the corner of her eye that Lewis had turned his head, and was looking at her.

Their glances met, meshed; blue eyes blazing into grey. Every never-ending in her body burst into painful life. It had been like that all those years ago. He had looked at her then with those amazing blue eyes, and then ...

But then the look in his eyes had been one of admiration; or arousal and eagerness. Now it was one of...

Of what? she asked herself dizzily as she tried to look away. Absently she wondered why—when his body had so obviously matured from the slight thinness of his early twenties as though now he had finally grown into the height and breadth of the bone-structure nature had given him—his face seemed so much more sharply sculptured, so much harder, so much more shockingly masculine. He had never been good-looking in the almost too handsome fashion of a film star, but he had always had a potent, very unnerving almost—at least to her—aura of male sexuality which time seemed to have enhanced rather than lessened; and yet there was nothing overtly sexual about him. He was wearing a well-tailored plain navy suit, a crisp white shirt and a suitably discreet tie, his clothes very similar in fact to those worn by both Ian and Tony, and yet on *him*...

The slight movement of his body re-attracted her attention, her glance flicking helplessly towards it so that she was gut-wrenchingly conscious of the power of the muscles that lay beneath his skin, achingly aware of his body, his maleness, in a way she hadn't been aware of a man's physical masculinity in years.

'I . . . I must go,' she reiterated huskily. 'I promised I'd go round and see Michael.'

'But I thought we were going to finalise the formal winding down of the appeal,' Ian protested. 'I——'

'I'm sorry, Ian. I . . . I can't stay. Not now!'

She was almost gabbling now as she headed for the door, desperately conscious of the way Lewis was watching her, and desperately anxious to escape from the room before she panicked completely. She knew that her behaviour must, to Ian at least, seem totally out of character, totally immature and illogical, and that as such it must be completely bewildering him. Later she would have to apologise to him . . . to make some kind of amends for what she was doing, but if she stayed in this room with Lewis even one second longer. . .

She shuddered, acknowledging how, for one heartbeat, she had been horrendously tempted to close the gap between them; to walk up to him and be at his side as though it was her right to be there.

That had shocked and frightened her even more than her sexual awareness of him. He had hurt her so badly that she had believed that nothing would ever make her forget that pain, and yet in the space of a handful of heartbeats she had found herself recklessly, dangerously ignoring reality and allowing herself to pretend that they were still together . . . a couple . . . a pair . . . that they were still . . . still what? she asked herself sickly as she pulled open the door and walked through it. Still lovers?

The wave of heat that suffused her told its own betraying story.

Ian, who had followed her through the door and who was now reaching out to delay her, asked anxiously, 'Is everything all right? You seem . . . different, somehow. I . . .'

'I'm fine, Ian. It's just that I feel so guilty about forgetting I had promised to see Michael today. I only remembered when I was halfway here, so it seemed simpler to explain in person.'

She had never known she possessed such a facility for fiction . . . for lying.

'I'll ring you tomorrow about the appeal. I . . . I am sorry.'

He was smiling at her, still quite obviously concerned, but, being the man he was, he made no attempt to restrain or question her, and it was only once she had reached the sanctuary of her car that she realised that she still had no idea what on earth Lewis was doing in town, nor, more importantly, how long he intended to stay.

To judge from his shock at seeing her, if he had had any intentions of staying on he must surely now have changed his mind, she reflected grimly and self-punishingly. Thank goodness Jessica was back at university!

Jessica. She felt sick inside. How would she feel if she knew that her father had been here in town and she, her mother, had not said one word to alert her? But Jessica had never expressed any desire to try and track down her father.

That did not mean that somewhere, buried deep inside her, there wasn't a very natural desire to know more about him. She would hardly have been human if she had ever experienced *that* emotion, that need, even if loyalty to her mother had kept her silent on the subject.

As she sat in the car, knowing that she was still too shocked to drive, Lacey leaned her head back against the neck-rest and acknowledged wearily that she was now in danger of adding guilt to all her emotional burdens.

It was a long time before she felt physically and emotionally able to start her car and drive home. When she did, her fingers were over-tight on the wheel, a frown of concentration furrowing her forehead, and she tried desperately not to let her mental images of Lewis come between her and her driving.

If she could react so horrendously to simply seeing him, she could barely endure the thought of what might have happened had he actually touched her.

Touched her! A small hysterical sound bubbled up in her throat. The last time he had touched her had been the last time he made love to her; less than a week before he had told her that their marriage was over.

She trembled violently, her eyes clouded with tears; only the blaring of another driver's car horn bringing her sharply back to reality and her responsibility as a driver to pay attention to what she was doing.

CHAPTER THREE

WHEN Lacey got home she was actually trembling in a physical reaction to her shocked and confused emotions. She went straight upstairs, sluicing her overheated flesh with cold water, trying to jolt her body back to normality and at the same time to quench the disturbing heat twisting her insides.

How on earth was she going to explain her ridiculous behaviour to Ian? She had lied to him, a lie so obvious and ill-judged that she was sure he must have known it, and she abhorred deceit of any kind—a legacy from the past, from the knowledge that, even as he had made love to her, Lewis must have been thinking of that other woman; the woman she had never seen but whom she had known existed and for some time, for surely a man did not simply fall out of love with one woman and into love with another in the space of a single week, and she could have sworn that when he was making love to her there had been love as well as desire and passion in his touch...his possession of her.

For a long, long time after he had left her, she had not allowed herself to think about that particular betrayal; her pregnancy had helped, keeping at bay those kinds of self-destructive thoughts, but eventually there had come a time, a day when, long after Jessica's birth, her thoughts, her time were not totally and completely absorbed by the responsibility and joy of her new daughter, and she had wondered then in revulsion and pain how Lewis had been able to make love to her with so much passion and apparent sincerity, with so much intensity and counterfeit love, when only days later he had shuddered back from her in physical revulsion, abhorring her briefest touch, the imploring plea of the hand she had stretched out towards him while she'd begged him to explain, to help her understand how his love could have died, how he could possibly tell her that he no longer loved her: that their marriage was over.

That was when they had begun, those tormenting, shocking dreams where she relived over and over again their physical communion. In those dreams there were no barriers, no pain, no sense of reality, only a shimmering, ecstatic kaleidoscope of remembered pleasures and delights, but in the morning had come the reality, the pain, and the guilt that she should continue to dream so idiotically and pathetically about a man who had forgotten her years ago.

She rang Michael's mother, asking if she could possibly go round to see Michael earlier than they had originally arranged, so that she could at least give her lie to Ian some form of substance.

The time she spent with Michael and his family as always left her feeling both spiritually uplifted and at the same time humbled, achingly conscious of the sheer purity and shining strength that the small boy evidenced, and yet heartbreakingly aware of the mortal frailty of his physical body.

Michael was in remission, the devastating effects of his condition halted—for the time being. For the time being, but not forever ...

Being with the Sullivans should have brought her own self-indulgent emotional problems into their true perspective, she told herself later on her way home, but instead she hadn't been able to help contrasting the closeness between Michael's parents, their shared love for their child, for their other children, with her own solitary state. They, for all the despair and heartache they had suffered, had something she had been denied.

At eighteen and twenty-one, she was fully prepared to admit now, she and Lewis had been too young to get married, and yet it had been at Lewis's insistence that they had done so, not hers. She had been living in a hostel then with other girls in the same situation as herself. Lewis had had his own flat. His mother had died when he was nineteen, their orphaned states being something they had in common. Lacey had learned that his parents had divorced when he was very, very young and that he could barely remember his father, who had apparently emigrated immediately after the divorce. His mother had gone back to live with her parents, who had welcomed both her and her child. In contrast to hers, Lewis's upbringing had been a comfortable, protected one, and yet he had seemed to know instinctively how much her own aloneness had hurt her.

He had shared her desire for a large family, for children, teasing her that the reason he was insisting on marrying her so quickly was because he was in a hurry to start his own dynasty. They had laughed a lot together in those days, or so it seemed in retrospect.

They had married very quietly—a church ceremony, something they had both wanted. He had taken her on honeymoon to Italy, a small secluded villa on a hilltop, overlooking the sea. She had woken every morning to the warmth of the sun against her closed eyelids, and the warmth of Lewis's hands and mouth against her skin.

When she tried to let herself into her house she was trembling so much that she dropped the key.

She could hear the phone ringing, but by the time she had unlocked the door it had stopped.

It was probably Ian, she told herself, ringing to discover what on earth had prompted her earlier behaviour.

Her head was aching, the tormenting dull pain that warned of an impending migraine. She had thankfully suffered from them less and less as the years had gone by and now had enough experience of them to know that the best thing she could do, the only thing she could do in fact, was to take her medication immediately and then go upstairs and lie down.

Hopefully in that way she might just be able to avert a full-blown attack.

No need to ask what had brought on this: stress...anxiety...call it what you liked, she knew it was as a direct result of having seen Lewis.

Her mouth twisted as she went upstairs and removed her tablets from her bathroom cabinet. They were on the top shelf and she had to stretch on tiptoe to reach them. Old habits died hard, and she still continued to observe the same rules of safety now that she had done when Jessica was only a small child. These days Jessica was the one who could reach into the highest cupboards while she needed to find a stool. Jessica... Her hand shook as she poured herself a glass of water. Whatever pain Lewis had caused her, Lacey had never been able to forget that he had given her one of her life's most precious gifts—her daughter... their daughter.

She closed her eyes, tormented by the memory of the slurred warmth of his voice, thick with passion, his breath dragging erotically against her bare skin, her tight swollen nipples as he had told her softly, 'Girls... I want girls... at least half a dozen daughters, all of them exactly like their delicious, desirable mama.'

'What if we only have boys?' she had protested, drugged on the intoxication of their love... their desire... on the sensuality he had shown her that she possessed and had given her licence to enjoy and indulge.

'Then we'll just have to keep on trying, won't we?' he had told her softly, and then his mouth had captured the tantalising peak of her breasts and all meaningful conversation had ceased for a very, very long time.

It was the sensation of the glass slipping from her fingers that brought her back to reality; that and the ache of anguish tormenting her throat, the pulse of all too easily recognisable desire invading her body.

That memory was over twenty years old and yet it was as clear and sharply cut as though it had happened only yesterday.

What was the matter with her that she was still almost obsessed with a man she ought to have dismissed from her mind and her heart years ago? Why was it that, even knowing that her image of Lewis had been a false one, that all the tenderness, all the love, all the care he had shown her had been nothing more than an illusion, she still so stubbornly persisted in using those early days with him as a measuring stick against which she judged the other men, kind gentle men like Tony and Ian, who wanted her to allow them into her life? Was it because she knew that no man could ever come anywhere close to measuring up to such impossible and idealised memories, and that their failure to do so meant that she would be safe, safe from the experience of believing herself loved, only to turn round and discover that she was wrong?

Perhaps it would have been better if she could have hated Lewis; but that solace had been denied her. Instead she had suffered anguish and loss and the most viciously self-destructive sense of failure and shame; a deep-seated and very hard to eradicate belief that she had somehow not been worthy of being loved; that she had been a failure as a woman.

Over the years she had managed to get these self-destructive feelings virtually under control. Virtually. Another reason why she had been wary of becoming involved in another relationship. She had been afraid to trust her own judgement, afraid to allow herself to believe that anyone could love her, just in case the same thing happened again.

After all, wasn't it true that there were people, women in the main, who seemed to love self-destructively over and over again?

Her head was starting to pound as the tension in her muscles locked her veins. She went into her bedroom, quickly stripping down to her under-wear, force of habit making her fold her discarded clothes before curling up on top of the duvet.

It was hot up here in the bedroom, vague sounds from outside drifting in through the open win-dow, its curtains closed against the bright sun-light.

The tablets were slow to take effect, and for a long time Lacey seemed to drift in and out of an uneasy sleep permeated by sharply focused memories of the past, of Lewis.

She fought against them, a frown marring the smoothness of her forehead, her body tensing in rejection of what she knew subconsciously lay waiting for her if she succumbed to the lure of her dreams. In them she could walk through a door-way that led back to the past; in them she could relive those precious shared hours when she had believed herself loved, cherished, desired; but be-yond her dreams and their brief panacea lay real-ity and pain.

Nevertheless when the pills finally took effect she instinctively turned to one side, as though curving her body into that of an unseen partner who shared her bed.

Memories drifted in and out of her mind, whispering silken promises, and her body started to relax. Once many, many years ago she and Lewis had shared a long sunny afternoon in bed together.

It had been a Saturday. He had been at work in the morning and had returned in time for lunch. She had been working in the garden and had gone upstairs to shower and change. He had followed her, walking into the bathroom just as she was emerging from the shower, whatever he had been about to ask her forgotten as he'd watched the way the small beads of moisture rolled down over her skin.

She had looked at him and known with a tiny thrill of feminine elation just what was going through his mind. She had been proud of her body then, proud of her ability to arouse him, innocently believing in the fiction of their love.

She had deliberately, provocatively almost, let the towel slip from her hands and walked towards him.

He smelled of heat and the dry dustiness of an office environment, these scents clinging to his skin, mingling with its unmistakable maleness so that she received a faintly shocking charge of erotic awareness in the contrasting hot, alien scent of man and the outside world, and her own clean, cool, enclosed woman smell.

'What would you like for lunch?'

She looked at his mouth as she asked the question, her voice carefully neutral but her body openly displaying that the preparation of a meal was the last thing on her mind.

He, as she had known he would, reached for her, running his hands quickly over her still damp skin, and then less quickly as he held her slightly away from him, repaying her teasing with a little deliberate torment of his own, while he pretended to consider her question.

But all the time she was aware of his arousal, of her own growing, heady awareness that she only had to reach out and touch him, that she only had to lean forward and stroke his mouth with the tip of her tongue...

It shocked her a little that she should feel this heady, almost wanton pleasure in her sleek feminine nakedness, her skin cool and soft, while beneath her fingertips, beneath the crisp cotton of his white shirt sleeves his body burned with heat and the restless, surging male urgency which she was deliberately trying to incite.

Shamefully she knew how much she liked to tease him like this, to revel in the security their relationship gave her, his love gave her, to torment him a little so that he fought to hold on to his self-control.

He was never violent with her, never aggressive, never anything other than a generous, almost protective lover, who always seemed to place her own needs above his own; and yet sometimes, when she opened her eyes and looked into his, she saw such an intensity of passion there, such a fierce heat of desire that her heart and her body would clench on a tight wave of awe and excitement that such an ordinary person as herself could arouse him to such emotions.

The sex lessons she had received at school, even the overheard conversations of other girls as she'd grown older, had warned her that it might not be possible for her to feel like this, to derive so much sensual and emotional pleasure from seeing and feeling the intensity of his need for her.

Although she had never told him so, never voiced such deep emotions out loud, the fact that he was prepared to betray to her how much he loved and wanted her, the fact that he allowed her to see how vulnerable she could make him, made her feel stronger, happier than she had ever believed she could feel, banishing all the years when she had been alone, afraid that no one would ever love her, suffering the fears only known to those

who, from whatever cause, had suffered the loss
of parental love while very young.

Now, as he touched her, her body trembled,
vibrating almost to the sensitivity of his touch.

As he started to draw her closer to him, she
whispered against his mouth, 'Careful, I'll make
your clothes damp.'

'Then I'd better just take them off, hadn't I?'

It was a familiar game, one Lacey enjoyed
playing, dragging it out a little further as she
protested untruthfully, 'But what about lunch?
I'm hungry...'

'You want to get dressed?'

His hand was cupping her breast. The previous
weekend he had been putting a new fence around
the garden, and his skin was still callused from the
outdoor work. She liked the sensation of his hard
skin against her softness, rubbing herself
sinuously against him to increase the sensation of
pleasure, while responding, 'Mm...I suppose I
should.'

His shirt was unfastened at the neck, and if she
stood on tiptoe she could just about manage to
kiss his throat, letting her lips absorb the hot, salty
taste of his skin. She loved the scent and taste of
him—it was something that was uniquely his,
something that clung to his clothes, to their bed,
causing her often when he wasn't there to stroke

her fingers against a shirt he had worn, a pillow on which he had slept.

He often told her that she was unbelievably sensual, and when he said it his eyes would darken with a passion that told her how much he enjoyed that aspect of her personality. An aspect which until she had met him she had never even known existed, and one which even now she kept closely guarded, secret, something she shared with him and him alone. It was as though their love gave her the freedom, the confidence to step outside the image she showed the world to share with him and shower on him all the gifts of her womanhood.

Now, as she kissed and licked his throat, she felt the familiar tension hardening his muscles, caught the familiar small sound he made in his throat, knew with eager joy that soon Lewis would pick her up and carry her over to their bed and that, once there, he would stroke her, kiss her, pleasure her until she was crying out to him, pleading with him for the ultimate expression of his desire, his love...but someone was knocking on the door, the sound overriding her urgent pleas.

Lacey came out of her dream, her body trembling and drenched in sweat, to the realisation that someone actually was knocking on her front door.

She reacted instinctively to the imperative summons, sliding awkwardly off the bed, picking up the robe on the chair and hurriedly pulling it on as she rushed downstairs.

Because of her headache she had forgotten to put the door on the safety chain, and now, as she opened it, it swung back so that the man standing outside frowned a little before stepping into the hall.

Lacey noted his brief frown with a tiny detached corner of her brain, the only part left free from the numbing, paralysing shock of seeing her ex-husband standing there.

'Lewis!' she exclaimed weakly.

His presence, coming so totally unexpectedly hard on the heels of her erotic dream memories, was too much for her brain to cope logically with.

As he closed the door behind him, she moved automatically towards him. Her body was still soft and warm from her dream, her senses still aroused by the memory of their lovemaking.

It didn't seem to matter that her brain, still struggling to recover from the shock of seeing him, was desperately trying to scream a warning to her body; the latter appeared to have no intentions of listening to it.

'Lewis.'

She said his name again, and this time the tremble in her voice wasn't caused by shock. Her hand was already half outstretched towards him, her senses totally bemused and confused by the

reality of him. She had forgotten to fasten her robe
in her rush to answer the door and now, as she
moved, it fell open, and in the shadowy coolness
of her hallway the light from the window on the
half-landing stroked the soft curve of her breast
with warm gold where the robe swung open to re-
veal it.

The fine white fabric of her bra did little to
conceal the dark silkiness of her nipple, still swollen and hard, still aching for the slow, sweet torment of the male mouth it had craved.

'I'm sorry; I had no idea you weren't alone.'

The harsh, almost angry words shocked her
back to reality. She fell back immediately, her face
hot with embarrassment and shame as she realised how close she had come to... to what? To
perpetuating the sensual myth embodied in her
dreams, to trying to turn them into reality by begging Lewis to make love to her?

Sickened, and filled with self-revulsion, she
quickly turned her back on him, fastening her robe
with fingers that shook and then folding her arms
protectively around her body, before turning back
to him and saying huskily, 'There's no one here
with me. What are you doing here, Lewis?' she
demanded. 'What do you want?'

The dream was gone now, and in its place was
reality. Her mouth twisted a little, bitterly. What-

ever had brought Lewis to her door, she knew it was not any desire to make love to her.

Was he afraid that she might tell people that they had once been married? Was he motivated by guilt, or fear, or perhaps merely by curiosity?

'You're alone?'

The incredulity in his voice made her tense. Now that she was fully awake she was beginning to realise just what kind of picture she must have presented when she'd opened the door.

Even at twenty-one Lewis had possessed a sensitivity, an awareness of the feminine psyche and its capacity for sensuality and responsiveness, which had often awed and amazed her.

Add to that knowledge twenty-odd years of experience and living, and she knew that he must have been immediately aware that she had opened the door to him in a state of acute physical arousal, even if that arousal had now vanished so completely that even she could hardly believe she had experienced it.

Or maybe it was more that she didn't want to admit that she had experienced it; that, twenty years on, she was still painfully and humiliatingly capable of being aroused by the memory of his lovemaking, even though she knew that their intimacy had only been a fiction on his part, that he could never have been as committed to her as he had pretended.

How many times when they had made love, when she had thought he was just as deeply enmeshed in his desire for her as she was in her love and desire for him, had he secretly been holding himself aloof from her, allowing her to believe she had his total commitment and love when she did not?

That question had tormented her ceaselessly over the years, making it impossible for her to trust her judgement where men were concerned, making it impossible for her to form another sexual and emotional relationship.

Had he ever realised how much he had damaged her, how much he had hurt her? Did he even care? But she didn't blame him. No, she blamed herself for being stupid enough to believe in him . . . in his love, when surely there must have been something, some sign . . . some warning that he was deceiving her which she had overlooked.

Perhaps he had even thought when he'd married her that he did love her; or perhaps it was only when it was too late that he'd realised that he did not.

She put her hand up to her forehead. Her head still ached, a dull tension headache, the pain slowly spreading down her neck and into her shoulder muscles.

As she half turned away from him, she heard Lewis saying, 'You still get them . . . those migraine attacks.' His voice sounded oddly gruff, as though there was some kind of constriction in his throat.

Her own throat tightened in response, pain welling up inside her. 'Yes, I still get them,' she answered, keeping her back to him. 'I'm sure you haven't come here to talk about my migraine attacks, Lewis. What is it you do want? After all, we both know that it can't possibly be me.'

Her whole body went tense with shock as she heard the bitterness, the betrayal in her own voice. What on earth was she doing? Did she want him to know how much the past still hurt her?

She heard him make a small sound. It could have been shock, it could have been disgust. She wanted to turn round and confront him, to tell him that there could be no purpose in his being here in her hallway, but she lacked the courage to do so, knew that if she turned and looked at him now...

'I came to talk to you about Jessica.'

Now she did turn round, her eyes confused and wary. Her heart had started to beat very fast as panic took hold of her.

He knew. He must know. He had guessed...or worked out...but how could he know? She hadn't even known herself when he had left her that she was pregnant, and even if he *had* guessed ... what did it matter now so many, many years later?

Jessica was hers . . . hers and hers alone, the panic inside her insisted, and if this man thought that he could simply walk into their lives and . . .

'Yes, Jessica. Your daughter—my daughter!'

It was almost worse than if she had been totally unprepared for it.

She felt a numbing wave of sickness reel over her, a nausea which began in her stomach and spread to every part of her body so that she was literally unable to stop herself from trembling and shivering.

'Lacey.'

He was coming towards her and she reacted instinctively, backing away from him, her voice tight with pain and fear as she half screamed. 'No, no! Not that! Please!' She was moaning now, not screaming, her voice broken and defeated, her face pale and haunted as she felt her pain turn in on itself and burn into her, and then she saw the shock in his face and realised abruptly what she was doing. She was a woman now, not a child. She was beyond, surely, behaving with such hysteria and lack of control. After all, what possible harm could he do to her relationship with Jessica now? Jessica wasn't a child who could be snatched away from her. She was an adult young woman.

Behind her, Lewis was speaking, his voice urgent, desperate almost, as he demanded, 'Tell me, Lacey. *Is* she my child? I *have* to know.'

CHAPTER FOUR

LACEY took one deep breath and then another. What was the point in lies and evasion? All her adult life she had prided herself on her honesty.

'Biologically, yes, she's your child,' she admitted fiercely. 'But in every other respect, no, she's my child and mine alone. You never even knew that she'd been conceived... never cared.' She stopped, furious with herself for allowing her emotions to break through her self-control so easily.

'I don't want to take her away from you, Lacey,' she heard Lewis telling her quietly, confirming what she had already known: that she had betrayed to him her great fear, her terror almost, that somehow he would seek to come between her and Jessica. 'That isn't why I'm here. God knows, I wish I didn't have to say this, but I wish she weren't mine.'

He wished she weren't his. Lacey stared at him in disbelief, frozen in the grip of an anger, a rage almost, so strong that it took her several seconds to ask herself why, when he had just freed her from the terror of believing that he wanted to make some kind of claim on Jessica as her father, she should feel this anger at his rejection of her, his verbally expressed wish that she wasn't his child.

'If you're worried that either she or I may make some kind of claim on you...' she began stiffly.

He interrupted her, saying, 'Don't be ridiculous,' and causing her to glare bitterly at him and challenge him acidly.

'What is it, then? Is it your wife... your children? Don't you want *them* to know? Are you so ashamed of us... of the fact that we were once married, and that I, your unwanted first wife, conceived your child? If you hadn't wanted me to have that child you should have been more careful. Only, as I recall it, you seemed as enthusiastic about the prospect of having children as I was myself. In fact——'

'I don't have a wife or any children.'

The words were so low, so filled with unmistakable pain, that she fell silent.

'Look, could we please discuss this sitting down? I...' He moved awkwardly, and she frowned, realising that he was limping slightly.

'You've hurt your leg. A...' Her response was instinctive, wholly feminine and nurturing, her brief movement towards him halted when he too moved, but back from her as though fending her off.

'It's nothing.' He was brusque, terse almost, rejecting her... again, she recognised, embarrassment flushing her skin.

'The sitting-room's through there,' she told him curtly, indicating a door off the hall. 'Please go in. I'll go and put the kettle on.'

She didn't particularly want a drink, but she needed time to assimilate what was happening. Her brain might have registered the fact that his presence here in her home had nothing to do with her as a woman, nothing to do with their past relationship as husband and wife, their past intimacy as lovers, but her body was rebelliously refusing to accept that same truth. Her body was...

Her body was reacting to his physical presence in very much the same way as it had done to her dreams of him, she admitted bitterly as she hurried into the kitchen and closed the door behind her.

Lacey's head was still aching, but the sick terror which had pounded through her when she had thought he'd come to try and make some sort of claim on Jessica had gone.

Strange how easily she had believed him when he'd said that that wasn't what he wanted, when

she had so little reason to believe in anything he
might say.

The kettle boiled, she made the tea, and put the
tea things on a tray. When she walked into the sitting-room with it, Lewis was standing in front of
the window, absently massaging his left thigh.
When he heard her come in he stopped, walking
towards her, taking the tray from her, asking her
where she wanted him to put the tray down, and
then, when she'd told him, complimenting her on
the room's décor.

'You always did have a gift for turning a room
into somewhere warm and welcoming.'

She stared at him, her eyes dark with pain, her
guard down as she registered the solemnity behind his words, baffled by the expression in his
eyes.

It was almost as though being here with her
tormented him in some way.

'So there's no doubt, then: Jessica is my child.'

The words were sombre, weighted. For some
reason the tone of his voice made her shiver.

She couldn't speak and so she shook her head.

'Then there's something I have to tell you.
Something I myself didn't discover until after we
were married, otherwise I would never . . .

'I have the same congenital disorder as Michael
Sullivan. I seem to have escaped suffering the
normal physical symptoms and disabilities suf-

fered by male children inheriting the disorder, but I *am* a carrier and it's more than likely that Jessica may be as well.'

Lacey started to get up out of her chair and to go to him, driven by an overwhelming impulse to do so, to wrap him in her arms as she had done little Michael, to cradle him against her body and tell him that it was all right, that she was there and that she loved him; and then she realised what she was doing and sat down again abruptly, her whole body starting to tremble, not so much in shock at what he had just revealed, but from shock at what his words had brought to the surface, had made her recognise; namely, that time made no difference at all, that her heart remained frozen in time, the heart of the young girl who had fallen so deeply in love with him. But she couldn't still love him. He was a stranger; physically familiar, perhaps, but in every other way...

'I know you must be shocked. I might have had twenty years to get used to the idea, but I can still remember how it felt the day I discovered the truth. I had no idea you were having my child. I thought...' He stopped. 'She'll have to be told of course.'

It took Lacey several seconds to realise what he meant. She was still trying to come to terms with his earlier bitter statement. What did he mean—

the discovery? How had he found out? Why had he said nothing to her?

'God knows, this was the last thing I wanted—to pass on to an innocent child my inherited taint, to be responsible for causing someone else the anguish... It should never have happened. If I'd known you had conceived——'

'You'd have what?' Lacey demanded shakily. 'Forced me to have an abortion...to get rid of our child...just as you got rid of me, your wife? If you felt like that why didn't you say something... why did you marry me in the first place? You said you wanted children.'

'It's a long story. I haven't come here to wallow in self-pity, Lacey. I couldn't believe my eyes when I saw you up on that platform and then again at the restaurant; and then today to learn that you had a child... an adult daughter——'

'What are you doing here anyway?' she interrupted him bitterly.

'I'm rather unique apparently. It's very rare for male carriers of the defect to survive to adulthood, never mind not suffer any physical effects of the disease. My specialist had suggested I might come here to meet Ian. There's some research being done on injecting antibodies from carriers into male children suffering from the disease. It's a very new form of treatment, but it seems to help put the disease into remission. The only problem

is it works only with antibodies from adult male
carriers, and there aren't too many of us around.'
He moved awkwardly in his chair, causing her to
frown. His leg. Was that why it was bothering
him? She gave a tiny shudder at the thought of
him in pain ... suffering.

'So it was purely by chance that you guessed
about Jessica?'

'Yes,' he confirmed. 'But now that I do know—
well, she has to know. There will be steps she may
want to take to ensure that she in turn does not
pass on the disease. Not an easy decision for a
young girl on the threshold of her life, but ultimately...'

Lacey's frown deepened.

She turned and looked at him.

'You're not suggesting that Jessica ought to
contemplate being sterilised, are you?' she demanded, outraged.

'It would seem the logical...the sanest course,'
Lewis agreed slowly, avoiding looking at her.

'You mean you'd deny her her right to have
children?' Her voice shook with emotion.

'I mean that I'd want to protect her and any
child she might have from the threat of pain...
suffering ... and ultimately death,' he told her so-
berly.

His words made Lacey wince and brought tears
to her eyes.

'It doesn't have to be like that now,' she told him. 'There are new tests...new methods. Jessica could choose to have only girls. How could you even *think* of denying your own child her right to have children?' Again her voice thickened with emotion.

'Do you think this easy for me?' Lewis demanded, standing up. 'All these years of believing, of thinking... As soon as I discovered the truth I had a vasectomy.'

'A vasectomy? But——'

'But you'd already conceived,' he interrupted her grimly. 'I didn't *know* that. Have you any idea what it means to me to discover that I have a child?'

'Yes, I think I do,' Lacey told him bitterly. 'And I thank God that you left me when you did, Lewis, because I think it would have truly broken my heart if I'd ever learned that you wanted me to abort our child. Thank God you never knew that I'd conceived.'

He had gone an odd, pallid colour that made his cheekbones stand out starkly beneath his taut skin, his eyes so dark that they appeared totally colourless. He was, she saw, a man suffering from acute shock, but she could not afford to have any compassion for him. Not after what she had just learned.

'Thank you for taking the trouble to come and see me,' she told him quietly, going to open the sitting-room door and standing determinedly beside it. 'I'll make sure that Jessica knows... everything.' Somehow she managed to keep her head high and her face expressionless as she added curtly, 'And now if you wouldn't mind leaving...'

As he got to his feet he half stumbled, and instantly pain flashed through her. She ached to go to him, to hold him... to tell him that it didn't matter... that nothing mattered... that she loved him; but she already knew that he didn't want her love, just as he had never wanted it or her. Just as he had never wanted their child.

'Lacey, please; you don't understand. I——'

'You're wrong, Lewis; I do understand,' she corrected him sadly. 'You hate me for conceiving your child, and I expect you hate Jessica too for being that child and for not being perfect. Is that how you feel, Lewis, that only perfect children have a right to be born?'

'Lacey, please.'

'*No.* I don't want to hear any more. Morally and ethically you've done all you need to do. I'll make sure that Jessica knows what's happened.'

'If you'd like me to be with you when you tell her...'

She gave him a bitter look. 'Why, so that you can take advantage of her and persuade her to be sterilised? No, thank you, Lewis. I've brought her up on my own and I think I'm capable of dealing with this without your help as well.'

She noticed that as he walked down the hall he favoured his right leg and she felt her anger drain away, anguish taking its place. Why hadn't he been honest with her from the first? Why had he married her when . . .?

He had reached the front door. He paused and then turned round, saying quietly to her, 'I didn't know any of this when we married. It was later, after——'

'After you met her . . . the woman you loved more than me . . . more than our marriage,' Lacey concluded bitterly. 'Well, I'm *glad* you didn't know, Lewis, because if you had known you'd never have allowed me to conceive Jessica and, no matter what pain you caused me . . . what misery . . . what anguish, I'd go through it all ten times over to hold Jessica in my arms the way I did the night she was born. That one moment made everything else that had happened seem totally unimportant. She was worth every second of misery you caused me.'

She opened the front door and watched as he walked slowly through it, his head bowed, his face slightly averted from her, but not before she had seen how strained he looked, and that something metallic or moist glistened in his eyes.

Tears from a man like Lewis. She smiled bitterly to herself as she closed and then locked the door after him.

Half an hour later Lacey was standing in the garden, without having any real idea of how she had got there. It was the shock, of course, she acknowledged while she frowned over the tightly closed bud of a pink peony with a concentration that really had nothing to do with the flower's unreadiness to open.

They had had an early spring without much rain, and the garden was bearing testimony to the unexpected bonus of early warmth and sunshine.

Later these same plants which stretched so eagerly towards the sun now would be wilting, scorched by that sun they had embraced so eagerly, longing for rain.

She gave a tiny shiver. So, too, did the human race reach out to embrace that which gave it the illusion of being loved ... cared for ... wanted ... and suffered the same bitter effects once it realised that what it had thought was love was merely a fiction, a cruel deception.

The scene in front of her started to blur and shimmer. She was, she realised, on the verge of tears. Shock again. She was aware of a frantic pulse of anxiety beating fiercely inside her, giving birth to an urgency that demanded that she do something . . . that she cease to stand staring uselessly into space and instead . . .

And instead what? It was too late to protect Jessica now. To keep her in ignorance of what Lacey herself had just learned was something she simply did not have the moral right to do.

Jessica was a very strong and courageous young woman, but to learn totally out of the blue that she could be the carrier of such an ultimately destructive gene . . .

Fear, love, anxiety, the need to protect . . . the need to soften the blow . . . to ease the pain her daughter would have to experience—these and a hundred other maternal emotions welled up inside her, and with them was another emotion: guilt. If she had known . . .

What would she have done—opted not to have children? Perhaps. Chosen not to marry Lewis in the first place?

It surprised her how instantly her heart rejected that latter thought. Lewis, the man, her husband . . . her lover. He had been more important to her than her becoming a mother. She had loved him too deeply to have turned her back on him and found another man . . . a man who could give her healthy children.

And yet she had wanted a family; they both had—or so it had seemed. She remembered how passionately she had talked about it. How often she had told him that in forming a family unit of her own, in having children, she felt that she might finally wipe away the unhappiness and loneliness of her own childhood.

Those had been the daydreams of someone who was still very much a child herself, she recognised now, her reasons for wanting the family she had declared so passionately was necessary to her happiness dangerously emotional ones.

And yet what would she have done if Lewis had told her about his medical history once she was pregnant with Jessica? Would she have chosen to go through with the pregnancy, to take the risk of giving birth to a boy with all that that entailed, not just for herself, but more importantly for that child as well? Or would she . . . ?

She moved restlessly, knowing with the wisdom that had come to her over the years that it was a question to which there was no clear-cut answer.

Knowing the anguish the Sullivans had suffered, she wondered if she would have had the courage to live through the terrible mental and emotional anguish they had suffered. She had been lucky: her child had been a girl.

And for Jessica it would be a little easier. She would have the choice of taking advantage of

modern medical science, and of opting to conceive only female children. Of not having sons...

Shadows clouded Lacey's eyes. It could never be
easy, simple, pain-free, and Jessica would carry
the burden of knowing that when she fell in
love...when she wanted to make a commitment
to a man...when she wanted to build a life with
him, to have his children, she would have to tell
him about her medical history.

If that man loved her as her daughter deserved
to be loved, as Lacey wanted her to be loved, un-
equivocally, without restraint, or hesitation,
without doubts or reservations, then there would
be no problem; but life wasn't always so easy...or
so kind.

She wished now that she had more time to pre-
pare Jessica, that her daughter had grown up with
the knowledge she now had to enforce upon her.

She frowned again, bitterness touching her
heart. Why hadn't Lewis told her...warned her?
Why was she such a fool that she still found it so
hard to equate the man she had loved, the man she
had so foolishly created out of that love, with the
actual reality?

Did she still really not understand that it was
possible for a man, a certain kind of shallow,
selfish man to claim that he loved a woman and to
appear entirely sincere, when in reality all he

meant was that he desired her and that the life of that desire would be cruelly brief.

When Lewis had said he loved her she had believed him. She had thought he meant that he would love her forever. She had been wrong. She was now, supposedly at least, a mature woman; old enough to have accepted long, long ago that the image she had created of him was just that—an illusion, an image without substance and reality. So why did she cling so stupidly to it...why did she allow it to stand between her and the opportunities she had had to form other more realistic relationships? Why couldn't she even now see Lewis as he really was?

If she couldn't hate him for her own sake, then she should at least hate him for Jessica's—for the inheritance he had given her beloved child.

But he had also given that child life, and so many, many times over the years she had looked at her daughter and seen in her feminine images of her father.

She tried to clear her mind, to think logically and calmly. Her heart was beating far too fast, she felt sick and nervous, the shock still driving the adrenalin through her bloodstream, sending her nervous system into panicky overdrive.

What would have happened if Lewis hadn't seen them and realised that Jessica was his child? What would have happened if Jessica had remained in ignorance?

She gave a deep shudder. She ought to be thankful that fate had intervened, instead of wishing in such a cowardly fashion that they had remained in ignorance.

She would have to ring Tony and explain that she needed to have a few more days off. She had plenty of holiday allocation owing to her, and they weren't particularly busy at the moment. Then she would have to make arrangements to stay in Oxford; book herself into a small hotel there. She wouldn't ring ahead and warn Jessica to expect her. That would only alarm her unnecessarily.

While her mind raced ahead, dealing with the small practicalities of the arrangements she needed to make, her heart was still beating too fast, her pulse-rate accelerating dangerously.

She wondered if Lewis had now left town. She hoped so. She didn't think she could endure the thought of many more contacts with him, of even seeing him. And not just because of what he had told her.

She hated the weakness she had shown when he'd left, when she had thought she had seen the betraying glint of emotion in his eyes, and contrarily blamed him for it... blamed him for still having this pull on her emotions... blamed him for still being able to make her feel compassion for him ... for wanting to ... to what? Protect him; spare him pain?

What a ludicrous thought—her wanting to spare him pain. She closed her eyes in mute despair. What was wrong with her? Why couldn't she feel what any normal, sensible, sane woman would feel in her shoes? Why couldn't she hate and abhor him? If not for her own sake, then surely for Jessica's.

It was only after all her arrangements had been made, after there was no possible reason for her to delay setting out for Oxford any longer, that she actually brought herself to acknowledge that she was deliberately looking for reasons to put off the moment when she had to sit down with Jessica and tell her what she had learned.

And even worse, when Lacey finally made herself climb into her car and start the engine, was the knowledge buried deep inside her that she would have given almost anything to have someone at her side during that interview, someone she could turn to ... someone who could support not just her but Jessica as well. No, not just someone, she admitted achingly as she set off down the drive; there was only one person she wanted beside her now, only one person who could lessen the pain both for Jessica and for herself: Lewis. She wanted Lewis. Her lover. Jessica's father ...

He had offered to be with her when she told Jessica, but she had rejected that offer, too proud to admit that she might need his support.

Too proud? Or too frightened to admit that she might want or need anything from him, that she might be in danger of repeating the mistakes she had made in the past of... of what? Of loving him.

She grimaced self-tauntingly. Had she ever actually *stopped* loving him? She was beginning to doubt it.

CHAPTER FIVE

LACEY arrived just after lunch, and booked into her hotel.

To her surprise, the receptionist on duty recognised her from previous brief stays when she had visited Jessica, and welcomed her with a warm smile.

It was a small family-run hotel outside the city in what had once been a large private house. The Victorian building was solid, its basic ugliness cloaked by the climbers that softened its walls.

Her room overlooked the gardens, where azaleas and rhododendrons were just beginning to be past their best.

She felt drained and slightly disorientated. In her bathroom she ran cold water over her wrists, hoping to shock her system back to its normal stability, but it only made her shiver.

She had no idea where Jessica would be—if she would be in a lecture or at home, studying in the house she shared with two other girls and two boys.

She gnawed on her bottom lip, wincing as she realised how often she must have been doing so when her sore flesh stung a little.

Perhaps if she drove over to the house . . .

The terraced house the students shared was only small, but, as Jessica had earnestly pointed out to her mother when she'd announced that the five of them intended to buy rather than rent the property, it would show a good return on their investment when, at the end of their university days, they decided to either sell it or let it to other students.

Lacey had been faintly awestruck by her daughter's financial perspicacity. This generation was so very different from her own, so very well aware of financial matters in a way she could not remember being shared by her peers. The money for the mortgage came not from Jessica's grant, but from what she earned during her holidays, and Lacey had only been able to blink a little and respect her daughter's acumen while at the same time worrying about her taking on a financial burden which might interfere with her studies.

One of the two boys who shared the house opened the door to Lacey, and told her that Jessica did not have a lecture that afternoon as far as he knew but that she had mentioned spending some time in the university library.

'She said she would be in for tea. It's my turn to cook.' He pulled a wry face, and then added, 'Would you like to wait here for her?'

'No. No, I'll come back later,' Lacey told him.

He frowned a little as he watched her walk back to her car, wondering what was wrong. He had only met her once before and on that occasion had been surprised by her obvious youth. Then later, when Jessica had talked openly of her birth and upbringing, he had been filled with admiration for all that both Jessica and her mother had achieved.

He wondered if he should perhaps have insisted on Lacey's staying, on offering her a cup of tea. She had, he recognised, looked very pale.

With time on her hands and nothing to fill it, on impulse Lacey drove out into the country, parked her car, and got out to walk along one of the many footpaths.

It was a silent, secret place; a place where nature was always on hand to reinforce the knowledge that it was she who was the true power that governed man and womankind. Nature. Man could never truly force her to his bidding but merely seek to tame her a little, to harness her power but never to control it. It was nature that was responsible for her being here . . . nature that was responsible for the news she must break to Jessica.

How had Lewis felt when he had first learned the truth?

How had his mother felt when she had found out? His mother. Lewis had once told her that his relationship with his mother had been far from easy; that she had never allowed him the closeness with her that he had sometimes craved. She had been a very withdrawn person, he had told Lacey, and as he himself had matured he had often wondered if her withdrawal from him had been caused by the divorce between her and his father.

She had never remarried, choosing to remain alone, either because she had still loved his father, as Lacey had always believed, or because she had dreaded having another child...another son.

And Lewis's father; he had deserted his wife and child when Lewis was very young; had, according to Lewis, emigrated to Australia, where he had effectively disappeared.

With the sensitivity of a woman in love, Lacey had guessed how much his desertion had hurt Lewis, and had tentatively suggested that, now that he was adult, it might be time for him to lay the ghosts of his past, to try to trace his father.

Privately she had not been able to imagine how any parent could turn his or her back on their child. Not then. And she had been quietly convinced that Lewis's father would welcome an approach from his adult son, had privately believed that it must be the bitterness in the relationship between husband and wife which had been responsible for holding him aloof from his child.

She had never known whether or not Lewis had followed her gentle urging to try to trace his father. Several weeks after that discussion Lewis had told her that their marriage was over; that he had found someone else.

In the distance, a bird rose from the trees, wheeling and circling overhead, its thin, keening cry piercing her self-control. She felt her eyes blur with tears, her throat close in a hard lump of emotion. She had never felt more alone in her life, not even when she'd discovered that Lewis no longer wanted her, not even when she'd known that she was pregnant.

There was no easy way of completing the task that lay ahead of her.

She glanced at her watch. It was time to go back.

She had timed her return well. Jessica was back. She came to open the door even before Lacey was out of the car, running towards her, frowning a little as she demanded, 'What's happened, Ma? What's wrong?' She stopped abruptly on the pavement as she registered the strain on Lacey's face, and Lacey felt her heart turn over inside her as Jessica suddenly gripped her arm and said quietly, 'It's him, isn't it? My father... Has something happened? Is he...?'

Lacey wondered if she looked as shaken as she felt.

'No. No, Lewis is fine,' she assured Jessica immediately, unaware of what she was betraying in the shock of Jessica's perception. 'I...I think we should go back to my hotel, Jess. There's something I have to tell you, and I think...'

'Come on, then,' Jessica said quietly. 'And, Ma, I think I'd better drive.'

It didn't take long to drive back to the hotel, both of them silent, both of them gravely serious as they walked upstairs together.

Once they were in Lacey's room, Jessica stood beside her and demanded huskily, 'What is it, Ma? I know it must be something serious. I've never seen you like this before. You look like...' She stopped and swallowed. 'If it isn't about him, my father, then...' She paused and joked weakly, 'You haven't come all the way here to tell me that you're pregnant or something, have you?'

Lacey shook her head, too heartsick to remonstrate with her. 'Let's sit down, Jess,' she began.

She went through it as quickly and as methodically as she could, telling her daughter everything that Lewis had told her, but omitting Lewis's suggestion that she might want to be sterilised, saying firmly instead that, while she knew it was a shock, Jessica must remember how many advances medical science had made, and that she mustn't feel that even if she did carry the malfunctioning gene it would not mean that she couldn't have children.

'No, just that I can't have sons,' Jessica responded bleakly.

For a moment both of them were silent, and then Jessica said huskily, 'What I can't understand is why he never told you this before. Why...'

Lacey shook her head. 'He didn't know, apparently.'

'How did he find out—about me, I mean? How did he...?'

Confused that Jessica seemed more interested in talking about her father than in discussing the consequences of what she had had to tell her, and worried that such lack of interest might dangerously spring from shock and a refusal to face up to reality, Lacey explained quickly what had happened.

'You mean, that was him...in the restaurant...the night...? *He* was the man I pointed out to you?'

'The good-looking one. Yes,' Lacey agreed grimly. 'I recognised him immediately, but I didn't think he'd seen us or recognised me.'

'And you never said. You never would have said a word if this hadn't happened.'

Lacey felt her heart twist with pain as she recognised the accusation in Jessica's voice. 'I'm sorry, darling. I was just so shocked. I . . .'

'You wanted to protect me from being rejected the way he rejected you,' Jessica said for her, her expression softening. 'I know you didn't do it out of malice, Ma. You're far too compassionate . . . far too soft and gentle for anything like that.'

'Jess, there are tests you should have . . . things we ought to find out . . .' Lacey pointed out quietly to her, trying to remind her of why she was here.

'It's all right, Ma. I'm not trying to evade the issue or to pretend that it hasn't happened. It *is* a shock, but it's much, much better to know now. I just need a bit of time to come to terms with it, that's all. You needn't worry that I'm going to pretend that none of this has happened . . . to push it to the back of my mind and bury it there. It's just . . . It's just . . .'

'Such a shock,' Lacey supplied huskily for her. 'I know that, my darling . . .'

'And he . . . my father . . . he just told you and that was it, was it? There was no mention of him . . . ?'

'He did offer to tell you,' Lacey admitted honestly. 'He . . . I think he was totally devastated to discover that you were his child. He told me that

he'd had a vasectomy. He...he also said that when
he married me he didn't know... didn't realise.'

'Did you believe him?'

Lacey shrugged her shoulders. 'I think I was too
shocked to take it all in ... When he demanded to
know if you were his child my first thought
was——'

'What—that he wanted to steal me away from
you like the gypsies?' Jessica teased with a flash of
her natural ebullience. 'I think I'm rather large to
be a snatched baby, Ma! Is he married? Does he
have other children?'

Lacey frowned. Jessica's curiosity about Lewis,
while natural, was making her feel very apprehensive.

'I... No, to both your questions. I've arranged
to take a few days off to stay here. I didn't know
if you'd prefer to arrange to have the necessary
tests done somewhere anonymous. Ian could of
course do them, but perhaps——'

'I'm not going to hide it, Ma, either from myself or from anyone else. And it is, after all, Ian's
field. I'd be a fool not to go to an acknowledged
expert. If you could arrange something for when
I come home at half-term ...

'My father—where... is he still in town?'

'I have no idea.' She started to tremble suddenly, causing Jessica to frown and focus on her.

'I'm sorry, Ma. I know all this must have come as just as much of a shock to you as it has done to me.'

If only you knew, Lacey thought, watching her. If only she could be the one to bear the burden for her, her precious child. She felt so guilty, so responsible, so helpless, and she also felt ridiculously resentful of the way Jessica kept on turning to the subject of her father. Always in the past she had seemed quite happy not to discuss him; had even said that she felt no curiosity about him, no interest in him, that he was not and never could be a part of her life.

'There's really no need for you to stay on here, you know,' Jessica told her, making her flinch with pain. 'I know what you're like, Ma,' she added more gently. 'I know you want to protect me, to make things right for me, but can't you see. This is something I have to sort out on my own, to come to terms with by myself. I can't use you as an emotional crutch for the rest of my life. This is my problem, not yours.'

Lacey flinched again, protesting huskily, 'Jess, I'm your mother——'

'I know. I know, but please let me deal with this in my own way, Ma. I promise you I'm not going to do anything silly. I shan't even go out and get drunk. It's a shock, but right now it isn't the most important thing in my life; right now getting married and having babies is the last thing on my mind. When the time comes—well, by that time I'll have got used to the idea. I do want children—but not yet. Don't think I'm trying to avoid facing up to it, though. I will have the tests done.'

She gave Lacey a fierce hug and said shakily, 'I'm sorry, Ma. I'm hurting you, I know. I don't want to, but I'm not a little girl any more. I know you're afraid for me, that you want to make things right for me, but please...try to have a little more faith in me...in the values you yourself have given me. Try to allow me to face this on my own.'

'Do I have to leave now, or will first thing in the morning do?' Lacey asked her, trying to sound light-hearted, but knowing that her misery was betrayed by her voice.

Now it was Jessica's turn to wince. 'Please, Ma,' she begged, and immediately Lacey felt ashamed of herself.

'I'm sorry, love,' she apologised, hugging her. 'You're quite right—I *am* being too protective. Very well, I'll go home, but promise me if you want me or need me for anything you'll ring me.'

'I'll ring you on Saturday morning, just so that you'll know I haven't done anything silly,' Jessica reassured her, adding, 'Look, come back to the house with me now. It's Mike's night to cook, and I think he's got a bit of a thing about you.' She grinned at her mother. 'He told me that you looked too thin. He sounded very disapproving, as though it was *my* fault. Come back with me, Ma.'

Lacey almost refused. The last thing she felt like was a convivial evening with a crowd of youngsters, but wisely she ignored her own feelings and needs.

This was the time to show Jessica that she respected her judgement, she knew she was now an adult, that she accepted her right to make her own decisions about the way she lived her life.

'Well, if you're sure there'll be enough food for an extra mouth...'

'I'm sure,' Jessica assured her. As she opened the bedroom door, she turned back to her mother and said seriously, 'Don't think I don't appreciate what you've done, Ma...or what you must be feeling, and don't think I don't realise how difficult all this must be for you. I'm sorry if I'm hurting you, but——'

'Don't say any more, Jess. I do understand. You're a young woman now, an adult. What *is* Mike cooking for supper, by the way?'

'Something with pasta.'

'Mmm...'

In the end the evening went far better than she had expected. Lacey even discovered herself laughing as she joined in the conversation around the table, forgetting for a handful of brief seconds what had brought her to Oxford, but then she would remember, and her eyes would cloud slightly, and she would have to remind herself that for Jessica's sake, if nothing else, she must not give in to her emotions.

It was gone eleven when she left, having refused a nightcap, and having thanked Mike for her supper.

'I'll be in touch on Saturday, Ma,' Jessica told her as she walked out to her car with her.

They hugged one another, and then Lacey got into her car. She would not cry, she told herself severely as she started the engine...or at least not until Jessica could not see her doing so.

For the rest of the week Lacey was tense and on edge, reluctant to be out of earshot of the telephone for too long, unable to relax properly or indeed to eat or sleep properly either.

The effect on her nervous system was inevitably adding to the stress she was already under.

By Saturday morning she was ready to acknowledge that perhaps it would have been wiser to cancel her leave and go back to work where at least she would have had to force herself to concentrate on her work.

All day Saturday she refused to leave the house in case Jessica phoned while she was out, and at four o'clock in the afternoon she finally gave in to the need which had been savaging her all week, and dialled Jessica's number.

It was Mike who answered the phone, greeting her warmly when she gave her name, but when she asked for Jessica he hesitated a little and then told her, 'I'm sorry, they're not back yet.'

'They?'

'Yes. Jessica's father picked her up this morning.'

Jessica's *father* . . . Lewis!

It was only later that Lacey realised that she must have replaced the receiver without saying a single word of explanation to Mike, but at the same time she had been so shocked, so disbelieving of what he had told her and yet also so aware that in some way his words had only confirmed a fear that had been hounding her all week, that she had been unable to articulate a single word of normal conversation.

She stood beside her phone, her whole body trembling. Lewis and Jessica . . . How? her heart jumped in sudden protective terror. Was Lewis trying to persuade Jessica to follow his own example to ensure that she would never have any children? If so . . .

She realised that she had curled her fingers into angry claws, that her whole body was tense with anger . . . an anger she wasn't sure was directed at Lewis alone.

Jessica was *her* daughter, *her* child. Lewis had had no part in her upbringing . . . in her life.

Sickened by her own reaction, she walked into her kitchen. She was *jealous,* she acknowledged shakily. Jealous of her daughter's love.

She had to sit down before her legs gave way beneath her. She felt horribly weak, her body a frail, empty vessel which was threatening to let her down with its physical weakness.

How could Jessica have gone with him? Surely she must have known how worried her mother would be when she didn't phone? Surely she must have realised she would ring . . . would find out?

There was a bitter taste in her mouth. What was she thinking . . . doing? She hated herself for the traits she was suddenly betraying; for the abyss which seemed to have opened up at her feet.

There was a mirror in the hallway. She found herself walking towards it, standing in front of it and searching her reflection, as though she could find it in some evidence of the horror she could feel, some evidence of the warped and bitter personality traits she was suddenly revealing.

How *could* she be feeling like this, she who had always encouraged Jessica to make her own friends, to have her own life, who had refused to try to tie her daughter to her with any kind of emotional blackmail, who had genuinely rejoiced in her daughter's independence of spirit?

How often had she heard her friends praising her for refusing to fall into the trap confronting so many single parents: allowing Jessica to become too dependent on her?

And yet here she was, sick with the very worst kind of jealousy, sick with suspicion and bitterness, and all because Jessica was with Lewis.

Lewis. There was a knife-twist of pain somewhere deep inside her, an awareness of great sorrow, an acknowledgement that, no matter how much it might hurt her, father and daughter *would* be curious about one another...would want to meet...to talk.

Although Lacey had never tried to hide from Jessica how much her divorce had hurt her, neither had she tried to blacken Lewis's name to Jessica.

People did fall out of love, she had explained gently when Jessica had been too young to understand the complexity of adult emotions and had asked why she had no daddy.

All the time she had been growing up, Jessica had insisted that she wanted nothing of her father. Had she lied...lied to protect her, her mother...?

In her heart of hearts, didn't Lacey acknowledge that it was only natural that Jessica should be curious about Lewis? Perhaps out of love, out of loyalty, she had suppressed that curiosity. But now, confronted by the necessity almost of discovering as much as she could about her own medical history, hadn't she had the ideal excuse...the ideal reason for allowing herself to get to know more about her father?

She tried to put herself in Jessica's shoes and had to acknowledge that, had her father turned up on her doorstep without warning, she too would not have been able to resist the temptation to talk with him.

No; the fault, the blame, lay not with Jessica but with Lewis.

He had no desire to come between her and their daughter, he had said. When had he changed his mind, or had he simply lied to her all along? And she, gullible fool that she was—that she had always been—had believed him.

Where were they...what had he said to Jessica? If he had said anything to hurt her...to make her afraid...if he had tried to persuade her to follow his own example and deny herself the joy of ever having a child...

She was, she discovered, almost wringing her hands as her mind fed on her fears, acting like a forcing house on them so that there was no room for anything else.

The phone rang. She snatched up the receiver, her hand trembling, but it was only Ian, telephoning to confirm that he had made arrangements for Jessica to have the necessary tests during her half-term break.

'She might not even have inherited the rogue gene,' he reminded Lacey gently. 'But of course it is best to be sure.'

She had of course had to explain the whole situation to him. Previously he had known nothing of her past, other than the fact that she was divorced. She had always had a horror of revealing the truth to others, of encouraging their pity.

'I was wondering if you were free this evening,' Ian continued uncertainly. 'There's a new restaurant, just opened——'

'I'm sorry, Ian, but I'm expecting a call from Jessica this evening,' Lacey interrupted him.

'Well, perhaps another time, then.'

As she replaced the receiver, Lacey told herself guiltily that she was being unfair to him and perhaps to herself. He was a kind, gentle man; the type of man many, many women would have been delighted to have as a potential husband; so why was she so unable to feel anything for him other than friendship and liking?

Sexually he did nothing for her at all. No one did.

No one. Again she felt that knife-like pain slice through her. She was lying to herself and she knew it. She had only had to see Lewis to reactivate all her old physical awareness of him . . . her physical longing for him.

It had shocked her how strong that longing had been, how sharp-edged and bitingly, searingly keen. Stronger than logic or reality; stronger than reason and self-respect.

As she waited for Jessica to ring, she promised herself that when she did she would say nothing about Lewis . . . that she would not react with jealousy and bitterness, with accusations. She must try to see things from Jessica's point of view, to remind herself that Lewis was Jessica's father and that the discovery . . .

What was she so afraid of, after all? That their shared medical history would give them a bond from which she was excluded? That Jessica would turn away from her and to her father, sharing with him her inevitable fears and doubts about the future?

At eight o'clock the phone rang again and this time it was Jessica.

'I'm sorry I didn't ring earlier, Ma.'

Was her voice different . . . guarded almost . . . or was Lacey looking for problems which did not exist? Was she being over-sensitive, Lacey wondered as she tried to sound as normal and natural as possible.

'I've been out...' Jessica's voice faded a little as though she had turned away from the phone. 'I... I've been with Lewis ... my father.'

Lacey realised she had been holding her breath, dreading Jessica's not telling her, or even worse lying to her. Now she felt both relief and guilt. How could she have so little faith in her own daughter? Why was she behaving so suspiciously... so... so jealously?

Her attitude wasn't only demeaning to herself, it was demeaning to Jessica as well. And to Lewis ... didn't it equally demean him?

'Yes; yes. Mike said you'd gone out with your father.' She tried to sound breezy, unconcerned, and knew she was failing when her voice sharpened as she couldn't stop herself from adding, 'I must say I was surprised that he'd been in touch with you, especially when we'd both agreed that it would be better if I was the one to tell you.'

There was a small pause and then Jessica said quietly, 'He didn't get in touch with me, Ma. I got in touch with him. I phoned Ian's secretary during the week and got his home address from her, and then I rang him. I'm sorry; I know how you must feel. I wanted to tell you...to discuss it with you, but ...'

But she had been afraid of how she would react, Lacey recognised bleakly.

NO RISK, NO OBLIGATION TO BUY...NOW OR EVER!

GUARANTEED

PLAY "ROLL A DOUBLE" AND GET AS MANY AS FIVE FREE GIFTS!

HERE'S HOW TO PLAY:

1. Peel off label from front cover. Place it in space provided at right. With a coin, carefully scratch off the silver dice. This makes you eligible to receive two or more free books, and possibly another gift, depending on what is revealed beneath the scratch-off area.

2. Send back this card and you'll receive brand-new Harlequin Presents® novels. These books have a cover price of $2.99 each, but they are yours to keep absolutely free.

3. There's no catch. You're under no obligation to buy anything. We charge nothing – ZERO – for your first shipment. And you don't have to make any minimum number of purchases – not even one!

4. The fact is thousands of readers enjoy receiving books by mail from the Harlequin Reader Service® months before they're available in stores. They like the convenience of home delivery and they love our discount prices!

5. We hope that after receiving your free books you'll want to remain a subscriber. But the choice is yours – to continue or cancel, anytime at all! So why not take us up on our invitation, with no risk of any kind. You'll be glad you did!

You'll look like a million dollars when you wear this lovely necklace! Its cobra-link chain is a generous 18" long, and the multi-faceted Austrian crystal sparkles like a diamond!

NOT ACTUAL SIZE

"ROLL A DOUBLE!"

PLACE LABEL HERE

SCRATCH HERE

SEE CLAIM CHART BELOW

106 CIH AKW6
(U-H-P-08/93)

YES! I have placed my label from the front cover into the space provided above and scratched off the silver dice. Please rush me the free books and gift that I am entitled to. I understand that I am under no obligation to purchase any books, as explained on the back and on the opposite page.

NAME _____

ADDRESS _____ APT. _____

CITY _____ STATE _____ ZIP CODE _____

CLAIM CHART

	4 FREE BOOKS PLUS FREE CRYSTAL PENDANT NECKLACE
	3 FREE BOOKS
	2 FREE BOOKS

CLAIM NO.37-829

It was time to control her own emotions, to make good the damage they had already done before it became irreparable. It was time for her to show not only generosity but wisdom and farsightedness as well.

Lacey took a deep breath and said as quietly as she could, 'He *is* your father, Jess. I *do* understand how much... how curious you must have been about him. In your shoes I'm sure I'd have done the same thing, and you do...' she stumbled a little and then managed to continue '...and you do potentially share a bond. Well, I can understand that you might rather have talked to... to your father about things... than to me. After all, he has a personal knowledge of the situation that I——'

'Ma, please don't make me feel even worse than I do already,' Jessica pleaded, her voice half choked by tears. 'It wasn't that; and as for any bond that might exist between us... You are my *mother*; Lewis...I can't call him "Dad"—I can't even really think of him in that context...not yet. I don't know why I felt such a deep-rooted need to contact him, or what I was looking for...' She stumbled, and Lacey's heart ached for her, for them both. Please don't let him hurt her, she pleaded silently.

Please don't let him allow her to believe he cares about her and then reject her.

'He's a very lonely man, Ma,' Jessica told her chokily. 'The woman he left you for...I don't think they can have stayed together long. He never mentioned her...never talked about her, but he never stopped talking about you...about——'

She had to intervene.

'Jess, it's all right,' she interrupted. 'I *do* understand. He's your father and I've never wanted you to hate him. He is, after all, a part of you, but you mustn't...There's no need for you to try and justify his actions to me. Our relationship, his and mine...it was over a long time ago. Your relationship with him is just beginning.'

They talked for another half-hour or so, and when she had replaced the receiver Lacey was conscious of a great burden of sadness which at the same time was edged with the knowledge that she had done the right thing in removing from Jessica any guilt she might have felt at contacting her father. The strain, the tension, had gone from her daughter's voice once she'd realised that Lacey was not going to protest at what she had done.

Perhaps this was one of the greatest gifts she could give her daughter, she acknowledged wearily later over her solitary supper—the freedom to openly explore and begin her own relationship with her father without the taint of any bitterness of opposition from her mother. Yes, she had done the right thing...but at what personal cost!

Tiredly she pushed her uneaten supper away from her. She felt both exhausted and restless at the same time, shaky with nervous tension, and very much alone. She looked at the phone, half wishing it were not too late to ring Ian and tell him that she had changed her mind.

Perhaps, after all, it was time for her to cut herself free of the past, to stop indulging in foolish daydreams of something that could never be, and accept instead the realities of what life could offer her. There was no point in wishing what was done undone, in wanting to turn back the clock to a time before Lewis had re-entered their lives...or rather Jessica's life, she corrected herself miserably. She ought to feel joy for Jessica instead of concentrating on her own pain. She had heard her daughter's voice, her happiness at discovering her father, and she could not, *must* not spoil that happiness. She must not let her own feelings create a barrier between them...a schism of misunderstanding and jealousy.

Ten o'clock. Perhaps if she had an early night... The weather forecast was good. She could spend tomorrow in the garden, working. The wooden seat needed a coat of preservative, there was weeding to be done, plants to be thinned out. Plenty of work to occupy her hands. But nothing to occupy her mind. Nothing to stop her thinking about Jessica...about Lewis. Nothing to stop her from remembering how threatened...how alone...how shut out she had felt when Mike had told her that Jessica had gone out with her father. She had experienced jealousy before; the deep, agonising jealousy of knowing that her husband, her lover preferred another woman, but never had she expected to feel jealous of her own daughter...to wish passionately that...

That what? That Lewis had wanted to spend the day with *her!* Her eyes filled with bitter shadows as she washed up, and then Lacey made her way upstairs.

CHAPTER SIX

For once the weather forecast was accurate. Lacey looked up at the cloudless blue sky and then grimaced as she glanced down at her stain-splashed arms and legs.

The stuff she had bought to re-stain the wooden seat was thin and runny. She felt as though more of it had gone on her than on the bench.

Luckily she was wearing on old pair of shorts and an equally old T-shirt.

While she waited for the first coat to dry, she went into the kitchen and made herself a cup of coffee. The house felt unnaturally quiet. She put down her coffee-mug, her eyes shadowing as she recalled the years when Jessica had been growing up and the house had been filled with her chatter, her tears and her laughter.

She had told herself long before Jessica had left home for university that she was never going to allow herself to become a clinging mother, that she must accept that one day Jessica would grow up and away from her, and she had thought that she had come to terms with this.

Now, though, the tears burning the back of her eyes told a different story.

It's only self-pity, she castigated herself mentally. You're just feeling a bit down because...

Because she resented the way Lewis was establishing himself in Jessica's life.

She tried to put herself in his shoes ... to imagine how she would feel if she were suddenly to discover that she had an adult child. She moved restlessly round her kitchen. She didn't want to feel sympathy for her ex-husband, to feel compassion for him and recognition of the very real shock it must have given him to realise that Jessica was his child.

Her life was complicated enough already without taking on that kind of burden.

Where was Lewis today? Was he with Jessica?

It was several seconds before she realised how damning it was that she had thought firstly of Lewis and only secondly of Jessica. She drank her coffee. She ought to be outside working, not standing here in front of a window, allowing herself to give in to what was becoming an almost compulsive desire to allow Lewis into her thoughts ... her mind ... her heart. She gave a convulsive shudder. If she was honest with herself, hadn't he always been there, no matter how hard she had tried to reject the way her emotions clung to the memory of him?

Those nights in which she dreamed of him. She was starting to tremble, to feel the aching, weak loneliness and misery that remembering how her life with him had once been always brought her.

She was a fool, she told herself bitterly. She was clinging to memories that had no basis in reality, to a love which had never really existed . . . at least not on Lewis's part.

Tears blurred her vision. She blinked them away. The garden seat would be ready for its second coat of stain by now.

She was just about to go out when someone rang the front doorbell.

Jessica. Perhaps it was Jessica, she thought excitedly, and then acknowledged that her daughter was hardly likely to ring the bell when she had her own key. Grimacing a little at her untidy, stain-splashed state, she opened the door into the hall and hurried to the front door.

As she opened it the sunlight dazzled her, so that for a moment all she could see was the silhouette of a man, his features obscured and shadowed; and then he spoke, stepping towards her and into the house as he said quietly, 'I hope I haven't chosen an inconvenient time to call round but——'

Lewis. It was Lewis. What on earth was he doing here? And then, abruptly, she thought she knew, and her initial shock gave way to sick anger as she interrupted him, choking back bitterly, 'But you just couldn't wait to come and crow—is that it? Well, you're too late. I've already spoken to Jessica. Why are you doing this, Lewis? You didn't want her... you didn't want any children. You said so yourself when you told me you'd chosen to ensure that you never had any... Biologically Jessica may be your child, but emotionally, morally, she's mine and if you think I'm going to stand by and let you hurt her——'

'Hurt her?'

She could hear the anger in his voice. It silenced her, shocking through her own anguish, making her pause and look at him. He looked haunted, drawn, ill almost, and as he moved she remembered the operation he had recently undergone, and even while she derided herself for it she couldn't stop the surge of weakening concern for him that overrode the shock of seeing him and the anger burning inside her.

'Hurt her,' he repeated less harshly. 'Is that really what you think I'd do?'

For some reason her eyes were stinging with tears. 'Why not?' she asked bitterly. 'After all, you didn't seem to mind hurting me.'

She went white and then red. What on earth had possessed her to make that kind of self-betraying statement? She held her breath, waiting for him to pounce on it, to deride her for it and taunt her with all that it had revealed, but instead he seemed to tense as though he had suffered a body-blow, his voice low and raw with emotion as he defended himself.

'I had no option. I——'

'You were in love with someone else. Yes . . . I know.' She felt sick inside. Discussing the past was the very last thing she wanted to do. It had been idiotic of her to make that comment in the first place. Desperate to change the subject, while she still had at least some control of her emotions, she turned away from him and demanded gruffly, 'Why did you go to see Jessica, Lewis? When you came here to see me you told me that your only concern was that she be informed of . . . of her medical history.'

He was silent for so long that she was forced to turn round and look at him.

He was watching her with a grave expression on his face. His eyes, so familiar, so achingly and accurately recorded by her memory, were dark with compassion and pity.

Anger stirred inside her, mingling with her pain and the burden of the knowledge she didn't want to have. She knew already what had really happened, and no matter how desperately she tried to push the knowledge away from her, she couldn't.

It was her pride that made her lift her head and grit her teeth to say shakily, 'All right, so Jessica was the one to make contact with you. What do you expect? Of course she's curious about you. Of course she wants to know——' Her voice broke and she had to stop. She couldn't look at him, couldn't bear him to see her weakness, but she had to go on, to prove to him that she didn't in any way see Jessica's behaviour as any kind of betrayal of her...of their love. She had to make him see that she was mature enough to accept, to understand.

Frantically she scoured her mind for something to cling on to, for something to rescue her, and then miraculously she found it and threw it at him, saying, 'You, of all people, should know that. After all, you wanted to find your father...to know more about him. You can't blame Jessica.'

'*I* don't blame her, Lacey. Not for anything. No, I don't blame *her.*'

The way he emphasised the last word... The deep sadness in his voice checked her.

'What are you trying to say?' she demanded. 'That you blame me...that I should never have had her? Well, it does take two, you know—just in case you've let that small fact slip your mind——!'

'Lacey, please, I haven't come here to quarrel with you,' he interrupted her tiredly. 'Look, could we go and sit down, and discuss this whole thing more rationally?'

'Like we did when you told me you wanted a divorce?' Lacey demanded recklessly. 'You're very good at being rational, aren't you, Lewis? Very good at locking everything away in neat little boxes, tidied up out of sight, when you no longer want them. As far as I can see there's nothing for us to discuss. When you came here to tell me...to ask me if Jessica was your child, you said that you had no intention of trying to come between us; of trying to claim her as your daughter.'

'What was I supposed to do, Lacey? She contacted me. Should I have rejected her?'

His voice was quiet and low, carrying a heavy undercurrent of pain.

It was that pain that silenced her. She wasn't a girl any more, rushing heedlessly into an emotional confrontation. She was a woman with the maturity to see that no problem was ever clear-cut and divided neatly into right and wrong.

She felt tears sting her eyes as the anger drained out of her, leaving her feeling weak and vulnerable.

'I didn't realise that Jessica had already been in touch with you. I came round to——' Lewis started to say.

'To tell me what happened. To crow over me——' She didn't try to keep either the pain or the distaste out of her voice.

'That's unfair and untrue,' Lewis interrupted her immediately. 'When have I ever——?'

'Hurt me?' Lacey gave a shaky smile. 'Do I really need to answer that one?'

'Lacey, please. I just wanted to talk to you...to see if we couldn't find a way of——'

'Of what? Sharing Jessica? She's a bit too old for that now, Lewis. I can't stop her from seeing you ... and even if I could ...' She turned to look at him. 'Don't you think I don't *know* how she must be feeling? What it must mean to her? How potentially damaging it could be to her even now if either of us...either of us tried to make her feel guilt over what she's doing? I grew up as an orphan, remember. I *do* know how it feels.

'I don't need you to explain to me Jessica's motivation for seeking you out. I've known her all her life, remember. But what I do need to know is why you're encouraging her.'

'She's my daughter,' Lewis reminded her huskily.

'She's been your daughter for the last nineteen years.'

It was unfair of her and she knew it as she watched him wince and the colour burn up under his face, but she couldn't afford to let her emotions sway her now.

'You told me you thought she ought to consider being sterilised,' she reminded him.

He looked at her, his eyes shocked and growing hard. 'And you think that that's why——'

'You're encouraging her...allowing her to believe you genuinely want to develop a relationship with her. I think it's part of it, yes.'

There was a long pause when the expression in his eyes both hurt and confused her. He was looking at her almost as though she was the one who was guilty of trying to hurt Jessica, when in fact...

'And if I was to give you my word that all I want is to have a chance to get to know her, to allow her to get to know me? She's not a child, Lacey, as you so rightly said. She's a young woman. Do you honestly believe that she'd allow anything I had to say on so important a subject to sway her judgement, especially when she only has to look at you, her mother, to see what joy and happiness having a child can bring? Have you really so little faith in the way you've brought her up?'

He was being unfair now and he knew it. She shook her head despairingly. 'Normally, no. She *is* very strong-minded, very independent... but...' She bit her lip and then dropped her guard completely, abandoning her pride, as she stepped towards him and begged pleadingly, 'Don't you see, Lewis? At the moment you're so new to her ... so special. It's like ... it's like a teenage infatuation ... a first real love-affair; your views ... your feelings will be so important to her. Please ... please don't try to persuade her to do something she'll have to live with for the rest of her life.

'You've made *your* decision. Please allow Jessica the right to make her own ... for herself.'

'As you're doing?'

Lacey bit her lip a little bit harder and bowed her head. 'If she should actually decide that she wanted never to have any children because of the risks involved, I wouldn't try to persuade her to change her mind. Not if I was convinced that that was genuinely what she wanted. At the moment I think she's too young—for all her maturity—to make that decision.'

There was another long pause, and then Lewis said slowly, 'And I agree with you.'

When he turned to look at her there was a haunted, bitter look in his eyes, and she wondered painfully what had put it there. Having seen Jessica, did he perhaps wish he had had other children ... other daughters ... children by a woman he had genuinely loved?

She could feel tears gathering at the back of her eyes and fought to blink them away.

Lewis looked tired, drained; he looked the way she felt, she recognised. He looked as though he wanted to sit down somewhere and close his eyes and let whatever it was that was weighing so heavily on him slip from him, freeing him from its burden.

Just for a moment she hesitated, torn between wanting to reach out to him, to nurture him in the same way as she instinctively nurtured everyone around her, and then she remembered the past, her pain, and all the reasons why she must keep him at a distance.

She glanced down at her stained clothes, and then looked pointedly at him and said quickly, 'Well, you've made your point now, Lewis, and I really must get on. I'm rather busy, as you can see.'

'Got the boyfriend coming round later, have you?' he asked her harshly.

She turned to stare at him, her eyes rounding as she demanded sharply, 'What boyfriend?'

'Jessica seemed to think that Ian Hanson has a bit of a thing for you.' He said it carelessly, derisively almost, causing her face to burn with angry colour and her small fists to clench.

'Ian happens to be a very good and a very dear friend. I am a mature woman who considers herself well beyond the age of having ''boyfriends'', but even if I did have I hardly think it would be any business of yours.

'I still don't really know why you came round here today, Lewis, but I would prefer you to leave now before you really make me angry.'

She was quite proud of her small speech, but Lewis didn't react to it at all.

'What I came round for was to ask you not to be too angry with Jessica for getting in touch with me. I know how you must feel about it, how little you must want any kind of contact between us. But I also know how much you love her and how little you will want to alienate her——'

Lacey couldn't believe what she was hearing.

'Do you really think me so stupid,' she demanded when she could interrupt him, 'or so selfish? No, if you want the truth, I don't want you in Jessica's life, but that's a personal feeling: *my* feeling. Do you really think I can't put myself in Jessica's shoes, that I can't understand how she feels? Do you really think I'm so selfish... so...so possessive that I would...?' She broke off and swallowed. 'And as for my being angry with her...' Her body knotted with tension. 'I'm not angry with Jessica, Lewis.'

'Meaning that I'm the one you've directed that emotion against.'

'Look, I just want you to leave,' she told him huskily. 'I don't see any point in our continuing with this discussion. You know where the front door is,' she told him pointedly, heading for the stairs. 'I won't see you out if you don't mind.'

As she walked away from him she could feel tears starting to sting her eyes.

'Lacey, please, I...'

She tensed as he came after her, catching hold of her arm, all the tension and emotion his presence was causing her boiling up inside, breaking down the barriers of her self-control so that she tried to pull away from him, crying out frantically, 'Let go of me...don't touch me!'

As she tried to jerk herself free of him he let her go. She stumbled awkwardly, blindly putting out her hand to save herself. Her hipbone collided painfully with the chest against the wall, but before she could fall any further she was suddenly snatched up off her feet, Lewis's voice harsh and angry against her ear as he gritted, 'You little fool! What's wrong with you? I wasn't going to hurt you. I only wanted...'

She was shivering, trembling violently as the heat coming off his body surrounded her. She could smell his familiar scent, see the dark shadow along his jaw where his beard grew. Her heart was thudding in frantic panic, her body aching...yearning. She tried to blank out what she was feeling, to focus on something other than his face, to blot out the effect he was having on her senses, on her emotions.

He might be holding on to her in anger and impatience rather than in desire; her brain might be perfectly well aware of that, but the trouble was that her body seemed to have difficulty in recognising this fact.

Her body. Her eyes burned with the strain of suppressing the tears; her throat felt raw and overtight. Every breath she took was reinforcing her emotional and physical awareness of him. She could actually feel her own yearning need for him deep within her body. Her breasts suddenly felt heavy and tender. She wanted to lean against him; to wrap herself around him; to...

Frantic with panic, with the need to protect herself and conceal from him what she was feeling, she twisted in his grasp, trying to pull away from him, trying to escape the enervating masculine heat of his body.

'Lacey, for God's sake, what is it? You can't really think that I'd hurt you.'

Her head jerked round, a reminder on her lips of how easily and carelessly he had once done exactly that, emotionally if not physically, and then confusingly she heard the pain in his voice. Unwittingly she focused on him.

She knew immediately that he had seen what was in her eyes because she saw the recognition of it flash through his own. She tried to pull away, to turn her head, an inarticulate sound of denial and panic strangled in her throat as he said her name, his hand leaving her arm to cup the side of her face, stroking gently against her skin, so gently that it was almost as though he couldn't believe he was actually touching her.

As she flinched and trembled he slid his fingers into her hair, his thumb brushing the flushed heat of her cheek, touching the corner of her mouth.

'No. Lewis. No, please, I don't want this,' she protested huskily, but they both knew it was a lie and that there was nothing she wanted more than the intimacy of his mouth against her own, his arms around her, his body... She wasn't even trying to free herself any more, simply standing instead within the shelter of his arms, still trembling, while his eyes gravely searched her face.

She was still helplessly trying to protest that she didn't want him when he started to kiss her, slowly at first, both his hands now cupping her face, his mouth lifting from hers so that he could look into her eyes, huge and shadowed with all that she was feeling.

She lifted her hands to his chest to push him away. Beneath his shirt his skin felt as though it were on fire. She could feel the rapid thumping of his heart, and her own body trembled in response. He was kissing her again, tasting the texture of her lips, his tongue caressing their soft outline.

Tears clogged the back of her throat as she fought to deny her own emotions.

How many, many times down the years had she dreamed of him kissing her like this, only to wake and find herself alone? As she struggled against what was happening to her, she tried to remind herself of all the reasons why she should stop him, why she should deny herself the intimacy her body craved. But even as she argued with herself her lips were clinging softly to his, and then parting, her tongue unable to resist the temptation of exploring his mouth as he had done hers. Its familiar texture and taste swamped her senses, the soft little moan of pleasure she gave drowning out the cautionary voices clamouring inside her. The hands she had put out to push him away had somehow or other slid over his shoulders, her fingertips trembling as she touched the familiar hard bones. The gap between them had been completely closed now. Beneath her T-shirt and shorts she could feel the heat burning her body.

'Lewis.'

She was unaware of whispering his name, only of the fact that his mouth was covering her own, that he was kissing her now with a fierce intensity that matched and fed her own need. She clung to him, opening her mouth to the invasion of his tongue, welcoming its possessive thrust with soft eagerness.

His hands moulded her body, urging her even closer to him. The heat and scent coming off his skin made her ache for even closer contact with him, to be able to touch him without the barrier of his clothes between them.

As a lover he had always been caring and considerate as well as passionate, and her body responded to him now as eagerly as it always had done, heedless of the warning cried out by her brain.

She wasn't sure which of them unfastened the buttons on his shirt, her only awareness that of the infinite pleasure it gave her to slide her hands over his damp skin, to kiss the hard damp column of his throat and feel the tremor that burned through him at her touch.

His hands were on her hips, holding her against him. She felt the tension in his fingers as he gripped her, and then he was caressing her, tracing the narrow indentation of her waist, cupping her breasts. She could feel her nipples pressing eagerly against his palms, seeking his touch.

'Lewis.'

She whispered his name achingly against his skin, need overcoming reason as her defences came crashing down, her body pliant and eager against his, her mouth trembling as she caressed his skin.

He tensed abruptly, and let go of her.

'Lacey, I can't.'

Immediately she was shocked back to reality, her own arms falling to her sides, her face ashen with shock and humiliation. What on earth was she doing?

She felt sick with self-disgust, immediately stepping back from him, seeking the protective shadows of the hallway in which to conceal the physical effect he was still having on her.

'Go. Just go,' she demanded brokenly, adding, when he simply stood where he was without moving, 'Go, Lewis. Can't you see that I just can't take any more?'

Her pride was in rags. She didn't care what she betrayed to him any longer. It was too late for that now anyway. He must know from the way she had responded to him how much she still wanted him. Tears blurred her eyes. She heard him moving behind her and turned round.

He was walking towards the door. He paused before opening it and then turned to give her one last look. She averted her head, unable to meet it. He had gone. She was safe. Safe. She laughed bitterly. Dear God, she would never be safe again.

She felt raw inside, still aching for him at the same time as she hated and loathed herself for doing so.

She went upstairs and walked into the bathroom, closing the door behind her. She was shaking so much she had to stand there for almost five minutes before she could move.

She looked at herself in the mirror and flinched at the image it threw back at her. She looked, she decided in disgust, exactly what she was—a woman who had been sexually aroused to the point where that arousal was plain for everyone to see.

There were, she discovered, tears pouring down her face, and she felt alternately hot and cold, her body convulsed with frantic shudders of reaction.

She turned on the shower and pulled off her clothes, dropping them on the floor with a gesture of disgust. It astounded her that she, who was normally so fastidious, should have wanted any man so much, never mind one who had hurt her as Lewis had done, that she had been oblivious to the paint-stains on her skin, the sweat that was now drying between her breasts, the general dustiness and scruffiness of her appearance.

She stepped into the shower, welcoming its powerful sting on her bare skin as though somehow, by punishing her flesh and subduing its physical ache, she could also subdue its yearning for Lewis. She scrubbed angrily at her skin to remove the green stain, ignoring the painful sensation it gave.

She washed her hair as well, ignoring the sting of the shampoo in her eyes, welcoming the excuse it gave her to let them fill with tears.

By the time she had finished, her skin was pink and glowing with the friction, and her hair so squeaky clean it sounded like a demented mouse.

She felt sick inside, her nervous system so knotted and cramped that she felt she would never be able to relax again. She was filled with shock and self-disgust, unable to comprehend properly what had happened . . . knowing that if Lewis hadn't stopped when he did . . . Jerkily she reached out for a towel to wrap around herself, missing it, and having to bend down and pick it up off the floor before she could tie it around her body.

She towel-dried her hair and then ran a comb through it, wincing as she tugged on it too hard.

She felt too exhausted, too battered emotionally to even think about doing any more work, all she wanted to do was to hide herself away from the world, to hide herself away from herself, she admitted with a small shudder, as she walked into her bedroom. Dear God, how could she ever face Lewis again?

She discarded the towel and crawled into bed, falling asleep almost immediately.

Her dreams were sharp-edged and uncomfortable, making her move restlessly and cry out against them.

When she eventually woke up the room was in shadow, and she was, she realised muzzily, not alone in it.

She turned her head to stare at the figure standing by the window.

'Lewis!'

She couldn't believe it.

'How...? What...?'

He came towards her. 'I had to come back. You'd left the door unlocked. I came up here and found you asleep. There's something we have to discuss...something I have to say, especially since it seems as though in future there may be some contact between us...as Jessica's parents. This won't be easy for either of us, but it may help clear the air.'

Lacey shook her head. Was she dreaming? Was this real? A sharp thrill of misery coiled through her. It was real all right, and it didn't take much intelligence to guess what had brought Lewis back...what it was he wanted to say to her so urgently. Oh, God, what a fool she had made of herself. Of course he had to have seen, to have known, to have realised how she still felt about him. Of course he wanted to make it plain to her that he was not remotely interested in her. Oh,

God, why hadn't she been more careful . . . more cautious? Why had she had to put herself through this?

She could see him standing beside her bed, watching her . . . no doubt dreading her reaction to what he was going to have to say to her.

Well at least she could make it a little easier for him, and ultimately for herself.

Without turning her head, she said drearily, 'It's all right, Lewis. I know what you're going to say. You didn't want me twenty years ago and you most certainly don't want me now. I apologise if I embarrassed you earlier on.' She gave a bitter little laugh, and then lied, 'You'll have to put it down to the contrariness of my female hormones, I'm afraid. I suspect that my body, after twenty years of celibacy, must have decided to go into revolt, but please don't take it personally, and I can assure you——'

'What do you mean, twenty years of celibacy?'

She tensed abruptly, furious with herself for her unwitting self-betrayal.

'Has there really not been anyone since me?'

She bit down hard on her bottom lip. For some reason something in his voice made her want to cry. 'Did you imagine there would be? That I would allow anyone else the chance to hurt me the way you did?' she challenged him acidly. The silence unnerved her, panicking her into adding quickly and defensively, 'Surely you don't imagine my... my body would have reacted to you the way it did, if I had... if there had been... if...?'

'If I hadn't been its only lover?'

The quiet words silenced her. She could hear him moving, and prayed that he would go, but she could tell that he was walking round the bed towards her, and she could hardly throw back the covers and walk away from him.

'I don't want to talk about it,' she told him huskily. 'I——'

'No, I don't think I do either.'

He was standing beside her now, looking down at her with that same grave expression with which he had regarded her earlier.

'You've been crying.' He reached out and touched her face, causing her to shrink back from him. 'Do you still want me, Lacey?'

The shock of it turned her rigid. She stared at him, unable to conceal her feelings. 'No. No, I don't,' she lied vehemently.

'That's a pity,' he responded evenly. 'Because I want you. I want you more than I've wanted anything or anyone in my entire life. Twenty years of celibacy *is* a long, long time, isn't it?'

She couldn't believe what she was hearing. It was a joke, some kind of macabre joke; it had to be.

'It's been a long day,' he was telling her. 'And an even longer week, and right now there's nothing I need more than to lie down and relax for a while, and since this is a very large bed, and since you don't have any physical feelings for me whatsoever, I'm sure you won't mind if I just lie down beside you on it for an hour or so, will you?'

He was getting undressed as he spoke and her senses responded helplessly to the sight of his body, tougher, harder now than it had been in his youth, more male somehow, more... more *desirable,* or was it just that her own maturity had made her so much more attuned to her own physical needs and desires?

She knew she ought to be doing something to stop him, telling him that this wasn't what she wanted, challenging him to explain why, if he was now claiming he wanted her, he had walked away from her so easily before; but it was already too late, her stomach muscles clenching as he removed the last of his clothes. She tried to look away and found she could not.

He was easing back the bedclothes, coming down beside her, reaching for her. Panic engulfed her. Once he touched her, once her body felt the longed-for contact with his, she would be lost, helpless to control her response to him.

'I want you, Lacey,' he was telling her as he moved against her, his hands stroking over her skin, making him shudder and tense as he drew her firmly against him. 'I want you more than I can find the words to tell you.' He kissed her, silencing her protest, whispering against her mouth, 'Let me show you instead, Lacey. Let me show you all the pleasure I've missed showing you all these years.'

He was touching her with hands that knew her body already; knew it and knew how to pleasure it, and she had no defences against that kind of knowledge, her frantic pleas to be released from her bondage her desire was imposing on her drowned out by the very intensity of that desire.

Lewis kissed her throat, her shoulders, the soft curves of her breasts, his hands shaping her ribcage, her waist and then her hips, holding her so intimately against him that she couldn't stop the way her body was responding to him.

His mouth against her breast made her cry out and rake her nails against his back, her body arching, enticing, inviting.

She could feel him looking at her and immediately she started to tense, suddenly acutely self-conscious and ashamed of her response to him.

She was a woman now, not a girl; a woman, moreover, who had borne a child. His child.

His hands held her waist, his dark head bent over her body. Shock kicked through her as he moved, his hands spanning her hips, his face resting against her belly, his voice harsh, almost tortured.

'My child. You've had my child. Even now... even knowing the truth, I still think I'm going to wake up and discover...' His voice thickened and she felt the dampness of his tears against her skin as he told her, 'Do you know just what this means to me? To discover after all these years... after believing that I'd never...'

She responded instinctively to his emotion, reaching out to cradle him against her, whispering to him as she had done to Jessica herself when she had been small, stroking the thick dark hair, feeling her body quicken with emotion as he started to press fierce kisses against her.

How often had she longed during her pregnancy for this intimacy between them, this shared joy in the child she had conceived? How often had she wanted this tenderness from him then?

'All these years, and I still can't believe it.'

His hand touched her thigh, stroking its silky inner skin; his mouth moved lower over her stomach and its tenderness was gone, replaced by a male urgency that made her clench her stomach muscles and try to push him away, panicked by the intimacy of what he was doing, knowing that once she allowed herself to experience the pleasure of that intimacy it would tear away her final shreds of self-control.

But already his mouth was caressing her inner thigh; already his hands were turning her, lifting her; already her body was trembling with expectation, with need, with the memory of the pleasure he could give her.

She tried to stop him, driven by an instinct for self-preservation, but Lewis wouldn't let her, instead holding her, caressing her until she was mindless with need, no longer trying to push him away, but moving eagerly against him, letting him give her the pleasure her body now so desperately craved, unable to stop him from knowing just how wantonly responsive she was to him as the ripples of sensation gathered and grew and then exploded in shock waves of release that should have left her satiated and exhausted but which instead seemed only to fuel her need to have him inside her, fulfilling some atavistic drive for a completion which she could only vaguely comprehend.

It was as though she had hungered, starved for so long for this one man that now there was no cessation of her need for him.

While he held her, and stroked her skin with soothing gentle hands, she lay against him, letting her flesh absorb the reality of him. Her lips touched his chest; it was damp with sweat. She lapped delicately at his dampness, tasting its salty tang, and against her palm his heart suddenly exploded into a frantic race.

'Lacey, don't,' he warned her huskily. His hands slid into her tousled hair as he held her slightly away from him and looked down at her. She could see the desire in his eyes, feel it in his body. He might not love her any more, but physically he wanted her. Where was her pride? she asked herself as she looked back at him. Where was her self-respect? *Why* was she letting this happen when she knew that he could only be motivated by a combination of pity and masculine lust, while she...?

Well, if desire was all he could feel for her, then let it at least be a desire which matched her own; a desire which would break through his self-control... as he had broken through hers; a desire which would make him cry out her name and cling to her, as lost to reality as she had been herself.

Ignoring his words, she bent her head and recommenced her sensual journey.

She could feel his tension as her tongue started to caress the flat hardness of his stomach. His hands gripped her arms; she could almost feel the blood hammering through his veins. He wanted her to stop... not to take her intimacy any further, but she couldn't.

It wasn't just for him that she was doing this, she recognised shockingly; it was for herself as well. *She* wanted this intimacy with him...

That knowledge shocked her, shamed her that she could allow herself to be so carried away by her love and desire for him.

She started to pull back from him, thinking it was what he wanted, but immediately he held her against him, inviting the intimacy he had seemed to reject earlier, whispering her name over and over again, his hands tangling in her hair, his body shuddering with need as he whispered to her how much he wanted the soft touch of her lips against his skin, the warmth of her mouth caressing him intimately. Her response was immediate, passionate, underlining her love, joy flooding through her at his response to her.

When he finally stopped her, telling her how much he wanted her, how much he needed her, how much he had missed her, she responded to him eagerly, yearning for his possession, welcoming its powerful, surging thrust, wrapping herself around his body so that he groaned out loud, filling her ears with his words of need and praise just as he filled her body physically with his body.

Later, sated and sleepy, she allowed him to draw her down beside him and curl her into his arms, her senses fulfilled and at peace.

She was on the verge of sleep when she remembered that there was something she had to say to him, some important point she had to make, some protective defence she had to erect against him.

She struggled to grasp what it was, and when she had, opened her eyes to look fully into his and said firmly, 'This doesn't mean anything, you know. It's just . . . it's just sex, that's all. Just sex.'

She shivered forlornly as she closed her eyes. What had happened between them should never have been allowed to happen. She ought to have had more self-control, more self-respect, but it *had* happened, and what she had to do now was to make sure that he never guessed that not only was he her only lover but he was the only lover she had ever and would ever want.

As she finally fell asleep, Lewis looked down into her face, his eyes shadowed with sadness.

Only sex. Was that really all it had meant to her? And yet, if so, could he really blame her? He had left her alone to bear his child . . . he had hurt her . . . denied her. It did no good now reminding himself that he had acted out of love . . . that he . . . that he had what? Made a tragic mistake. Would she believe him if he told her that now? Would *he* have believed *her* had their positions been reversed?

He remembered the way she had touched him . . . loved him . . . and he winced.

All these years and there had never been any-one else for her. It made him feel humble, and yet at the same time it made him feel . . . what? Very male . . . very proud. He grimaced to himself, a little shocked that he could feel such machismo at his age when he should be well past that kind of youthful conceit.

Soon they would have to talk . . . he would have to explain. Lacey stirred in his arms, nestling closer to him. He looked down at her, drawing her closer to him. When he had looked at her earlier and seen the desire . . . the need in her eyes, a taut *frisson* of sensation had raced through his body. She was so beautiful, so desirable, it seemed unbelievable that she hadn't turned to someone else. It couldn't have been for the lack of an opportunity to do so.

He had seen with his own eyes how other men reacted to her. Ian Hanson for instance.

A fine thrill of anguish pierced him, an urgent need to hold on to her and never let her go. If only she could forgive him . . . understand. His hand slid to her stomach and he remembered how earlier she had sensed . . . had known what was running through his mind . . . had known that he was thinking of the past, of all that he had denied himself in denying both her and his child. He still wasn't totally over the shock of discovering that he was a father, after all the years of self-denial and fear, after telling himself that he could never take the risk of passing on his own deficiency to a child—not for himself but for that child. And then to discover Jessica.

He moved Lacey gently in his arms and bent his head, tenderly kissing the smooth softness of her stomach. The evening sunlight touched her skin, highlighting the dark areolae of her nipples, still faintly swollen and erect. As Lewis touched first one and then the other with grave delicacy, she stirred slightly in her sleep.

Just sex, she had called it. That might have been all it was to her, but to him...it had been so much more, so very, very much more.

CHAPTER SEVEN

WRAPPED in a delicious, warm lethargy, Lacey came slowly awake. She was conscious of an unfamiliar weight across her waist, an unfamiliar presence in her bed. She opened her eyes and stared in confusion at Lewis.

He was still fast asleep, his jaw dark with an overnight growth of beard. His hair was tousled, one tanned shoulder exposed where the sheet had slipped away. He smelled musky and male, the scent of his skin sending small skittering sensations racing over her skin.

She felt too relaxed to move, too lazy to . . . She tensed abruptly as she heard a sound downstairs.

Someone was opening the kitchen door, and running lightly upstairs.

Before Lacey could do a single thing to react to this knowledge her bedroom door was thrown open and Jessica came rushing in, announcing, 'Ma, I'm sorry about going to see Dad without telling you first, but I——'

She stopped abruptly, her eyes rounding with shock as she focused on the dark head on the pillow next to Lacey's, immediately starting to back towards the door, her face faintly flushed.

'Jess!'

Beside her Lacey felt Lewis move and stretch and then sit up.

'Dad...'

Jessica stared at them both, her shock and embarrassment replaced by a wide grin.

'Well, of all the... And just how long has this been going on?' she demanded teasingly. 'What a pair of dark horses you two are! There's me, thinking... worrying that... and all the time the two of you...' She came over to the bed, her face alight with happiness, flinging her arms around them both as she exclaimed, 'Oh, this is wonderful... brilliant! I can't believe it! The two of you together!' She sat down on the bed, happiness radiating out from her, while Lacey stared at her in consternation, trying desperately to find a way to halt her excited chatter and put right her misconceptions.

She knew that, beside her, Lewis was now fully awake, but she couldn't bring herself to look at him. She knew that he must be feeling as shocked and disconcerted as she was herself. After all, how on earth did one explain to their obviously deliriously delighted daughter that, far from having romantically come together, they...

'So you approve, then, do you Jess?'

Lewis's wry question broke into Lacey's frantic thoughts, halting them.

'Well, I must say, when I walked in here and realised that there was a strange man in bed with Ma I was a little taken aback,' Jessica was replying mock severely to him. 'But once I realised it was you... Oh, for goodness' sake! How long has this been going on? And I knew nothing about it! It's so romantic after all these years... the two of you getting back together. When's the wedding?' She laughed. 'I hope you're not expecting me to play bridesmaid.'

Lacey was too appalled to speak. She had gone through shock, embarrassment, disbelief, and now she felt she was incapable of registering any more emotions but someone had to say something... do something before the whole thing got completely out of hand, and, since Lewis didn't seem to be going to do so, it was up to her...

She took a deep breath.

'Jessica, this isn't——'

Beneath the bedclothes, Lewis reached for her hand and gripped it warningly. 'What your mother's trying to say is that we haven't got as far as making any formal plans yet.'

'But you are definitely getting back together. Well, you must be,' Jessica said cheerfully. 'I know Ma, and there's just no way she'd be here in bed with you like this if that weren't the case——'

'Look, why don't you go downstairs and put the kettle on? Give your mother and me a chance to make ourselves respectable,' Lewis suggested, interrupting her.

'OK, I'll give you just ten minutes, and if you're not both downstairs by then...'

As she walked towards the door, Jessica stopped and turned back to look at them, tears sparkling in her eyes.

'Oh, I can't tell you how much this means to me—both of you together. It's...it's...it's brill...simply brill.'

She turned round and was gone, leaving Lacey looking helplessly at Lewis, her forehead creased with anxiety and concern, her own emotions, her own feelings of embarrassment and guilt forgotten as she worried about Jessica's reaction when she learned the truth.

Before she could speak, Lewis said quietly, 'Whether we like it or not, it seems that for the present at least you and I are going to have to play along with Jessica's belief that we're reunited and passionately in love.'

'No, we can't do that.'

'What do you suggest as an alternative?' His mouth twisted cynically. 'Telling her that, contrary to her romantic beliefs, we just went to bed together for sex?'

The brutality of it made her feel sick, filling her with anguished self-disgust. She had known all along that it was only desire, lust that had motivated him, but hearing him put it so clinically, so coldly made her want to weep with chagrin and despair.

'Is *that* what you want?' he demanded insistently.

Lacey shook her head, unable to look at him.

'Look,' his voice softened a little, 'I know this isn't easy for either of us, but we have to put our own feelings to one side and think of Jessica. It obviously means a great deal to her that we've—as she thinks—reconciled our differences and come together again. What harm can it really do to allow her to go on believing that for a little while? At the very least it will give us time to gently find a way of telling her that we don't think it's going to work out after all. But if you insist on telling her the truth...now...'

Lacey shook her head. How *could* she do that after the way she had seen Jessica react to the sight of them together? If she told her daughter now that they had just been indulging in cold, loveless sex... She swallowed hard. How could she do...? No, Lewis was right. They would have to wait.

'Shall I get dressed first and go down and keep Jess occupied? It will give you time to come to terms with——'

'With what?' she demanded bitterly. 'With lying to my own daughter... with pretending that you and I...?' She couldn't go on. Her throat was too thick with tears.

This was all her fault... hers and no one else's. If she hadn't made it so plain to Lewis that she wanted him... desired him... She felt sick with self-mortification, with guilt.

Lewis started to get out of bed. She turned her head away.

'About last night,' she heard him say, but she shook her head in denial.

'No, please, Lewis. I can't talk about it now. Dear God, why on earth did Jessica have to find us like this?'

It was a question Lacey was forced to ask herself over and over again in the days that followed.

Far from containing the damage already done, the fact that they were allowing Jessica to believe that they had been reconciled and were making plans for the future only seemed to exacerbate it. Jessica, it seemed, couldn't contain her delight in what she considered to be their good news.

Her original intention had been simply to come home for a couple of days, to apologise to Lacey for upsetting her and to explain why she had contacted her father without consulting Lacey first.

'It's incredible to have the two of you together like this,' she told them both over and over again.

Luckily Lewis had the excuse of needing to get back to his business to keep his stay with them mercifully brief, and so Lacey did not have the trauma of facing the possibility of having to share her bed with him for a second night.

She had had the whole day to spend with him and two more after that, when he had driven over to spend, as he put it, as much time has he could with the two most important women in his life.

The past was never mentioned. Jessica's excited chatter was all about the future, and the more she listened to her daughter the more despairingly guilty Lacey felt. Sooner or later Jessica was going to have to be told the truth.

Initially when Lewis had talked of letting Jessica come to terms with the realisation that the relationship between them wasn't working out, it had seemed a simple, easy solution; but now that Lacey had time to consider it and to realise that it wasn't something that could be accomplished overnight, she was beginning to panic that she would do something to betray the strain she was under, the pain she was going through, the agony she was enduring. Because it *was* agony having to spend so much time with Lewis, having to accept the small physical gestures of intimacy he made towards her, the brief kiss on her forehead, his arm round her shoulders, the small, intimate touches that reaffirmed Jessica's belief that they were deeply in love.

Deeply in love. Well, it was true of one of them, at least, and the problem was that that one was falling more and more deeply into that love with every day that passed.

No matter how much she tried to remind herself of the past and all that had happened, Lacey knew she was daily becoming more dependent on Lewis . . . more involved with him, so that she was torn between anguish and self-hatred at her own weakness and inability to face reality.

Fortunately Jessica was only able to spend a few days at home.

To Lacey's consternation, on their last afternoon together Jessica suggested that Lewis took them both to see his home.

'After all, I expect that you and Ma will be living there once you've finally set a date for the wedding,' she continued blithely. 'I mean, your business is there——'

'Jessica,' Lacey protested. 'I don't think——'

'That's all right,' Lewis interrupted her, 'and besides, Jess, is right, although I warn you that the house isn't anything like as...as home-like as this.'

He said it almost bleakly, his face suddenly shuttered, causing Lacey to worry at her bottom lip. He never spoke of her, the woman he had left her for, or of their time together. She knew now that he had never married her, but presumably they must have lived together, shared a home... plans...and she shrank from the thought of even visiting the house he had shared with another woman; a woman he had loved more than he had loved her.

'I bought the house five years ago,' he was telling Jessica. 'In all honesty, it's too large for one person. Much too large. I don't know why I bought it really.'

'Wishful thinking,' Jessica suggested, smiling at him.

'Perhaps,' Lewis agreed. 'Although I had no idea then that your mother...that you existed.'

'It's not too late, you know,' Jessica told him softly. 'You and Ma can still have another child...more children. After all, these days a vasectomy can be reversed, and Ma isn't even forty yet——'

'Jessica,' Lacey interrupted her quickly, but Jessica refused to be quelled, telling her firmly,

'Come on, Ma, you know you'd love another child . . . and I certainly wouldn't object to a little sister.'

The knowledge which all three of them shared was mirrored in those words, and, despite the grim look in Lewis's eyes, Lacey felt the familiar pang inside her, the familiar ache in her womb, reinforcing the knowledge that Jessica was right: that she would like another child, just as long as that child was Lewis's.

'If my tests prove positive I shan't let it stop me from having children,' Jessica told them both quietly. 'Not boys—I couldn't take that risk—but girls.'

Lacey tensed as she saw Lewis walk over to the french windows and step through them into the garden, his back rigid with tension.

'What is it . . . what did I say?' Jessica asked her bewilderedly.

'He's worried about you,' Lacey told her gently. 'Give him time, Jess. He feels guilty . . . responsible . . . for the fact that you will probably never be able to choose to have sons, at least not without the risk of passing on to them his defective gene——'

'But at least I *can* choose,' Jessica interrupted her. 'What would you have done, Ma, if he'd told you about . . . about the risk after you knew you were carrying me?'

'I don't know,' Lacey told her honestly. 'I think I would probably have continued with the pregnancy.'

'But Dad wouldn't have wanted you to, would he? He'd have tried to persuade you to have an abortion.'

Lacey bit her lip. 'Jessica, you've seen what's happening to little Michael. You know what his family has gone through. I'm not trying to say that I agree with Lewis's attitude, but I do understand it.'

'Yes. Yes, I know. I just suddenly realised that if you hadn't...if he hadn't divorced you when he did, I might never have been born.'

'But you *were* born,' Lacey told her, 'and, thanks to modern technology, *you* will have the choice of knowing that you can opt to have only girls.'

Jessica went to stand by the window. 'Dad looks so alone. I think he's missed you dreadfully. It's obvious how he feels about you, and I know that you love him...that you've always loved him. I'm so glad that you've come together again.'

'Jess, it isn't as clear-cut as that. Things may not work out,' Lacey began, but Jessica wasn't listening to her.

'I'm looking forward to seeing his house, aren't you? I wonder what it's like.'

Lewis was staring towards the house. Jessica opened the french window and ran up to him, hugging him with a love that made Lacey's eyes sting with tears.

Soon she would have to tell her daughter the truth. Soon, but not yet; not while her relationship with Lewis was still so new and vulnerable.

Driving through the once familiar environs of the town where she had once lived with Lewis made Lacey feel increasingly tense and on edge.

The town had changed over the years, had grown and spread out, but its centre was the same.

Lewis now had a much larger office in the town square. He pointed it out to them as they drove through it, responding to Jessica's excited questions by admitting that he now owned the handsome three-storey Georgian building in which his offices were housed.

He had, he explained to them, bought out his original partner some years previously, and had expanded the business so that he now had several fully qualified staff working for him, as well as an office manager and several clerks.

'Hear that, Ma? You're marrying a wealthy man, so hang on to him,' Jessica teased, but Lacey suspected that it was probably true and that Lewis was indeed very well off.

His car, his clothes and now his offices certainly seemed to bear out that impression. She moved nervously in her seat. Jessica had insisted that her mother sit in the front passenger-seat of the car, next to Lewis, although Lacey would much rather have sat in the back.

Out of the corner of her eye she saw the way he flinched a little as he had to brake unexpectedly for someone crossing the road. The removal of the bone marrow he had given for research in addition to temporarily weakening his limb had left a small scar on his upper thigh. Her skin suddenly coloured hotly as she remembered how she had smoothed it, kissed it, tenderly caressing the small wound. She started to tremble inside and hated herself for her weakness. Every time she thought about the way they had made love it affected her like this, making her body start to ache and her senses swim.

Lewis was saying something about its not being far now. She looked at him, focusing briefly on his mouth, her heart turning over inside her as she remembered its delicate friction against her body.

They were clear of the town now, driving through the suburbs and out into the open country, and they were, she recognised with relief—on the opposite side of the town from the area where they had originally set up home.

They turned off the main road into a quiet country lane. Lacey could see a drive ahead of them. Lewis turned into it and she caught her breath in shock as she saw the house.

It was a low white-painted farmhouse with red tiled roofs and lead-paned windows, surrounded by large mature gardens and protected by an encircling ring of trees.

'Is this it? It's brilliant!' Jessica announced. 'What do you think, Ma?'

Lewis had brought the car to a halt. Both he and Jessica were, she realised, looking at her.

Shakily she told them both, 'It's . . . it's . . . very nice.'

'Very nice!' Jessica scoffed. 'Oh, come on, Ma, you can do better than that.'

Lacey gave her a wan smile.

Once long, long ago, on a hot summer afternoon, lying with Lewis on their bed, the heat pressing down on the small, narrow row of houses, she had dreamily described to Lewis the sort of house she dreamed of owning...the sort of house just right for the family she longed to have.

From its exterior this house might have been designed to fit that description, and she was unbearably conscious of the cruel irony that Lewis should own it.

Five years ago, he said he had bought it, plenty of time for him to have forgotten the house she had described to him all those years ago. She reached for the door-handle of the car, suddenly desperate for some fresh air, forgetting that her seatbelt was still fastened.

Jessica was already opening her door and getting out, and Lacey and Lewis were alone in the car.

'I bought it because of you,' he told her quietly. 'I was driving past one day and I saw it.'

'And it just happened to be for sale ... and you thought, Oh, there's a house like the one Lacey wanted.' Her voice was choked with tears, bitterness thickening the words.

He was looking towards her, but she couldn't bear to look at him ... couldn't endure him seeing the misery and unhappiness in her eyes.

'No, as a matter of fact it wasn't for sale ... but the owners were an elderly couple and thinking about retiring to somewhere more convenient. I told them if they ever did decide to sell to get in touch with me.'

'You wanted it that much?' She was puzzled now.

'I *needed* it that much,' he corrected her, bending over her to release her seatbelt.

She could smell the scent of his shampoo, his soap; she could see the male graining of his skin. His head was so close to her that if she moved only slightly she would feel the warmth of his breath against her breast.

A deep shudder ran through her. Beneath her clothes her nipples peaked and hardened.

'Lacey, I . . .'

His hand was on her shoulder, his voice low and urgent. She had the oddest feeling that if she looked at him now she wouldn't be able to stop herself from begging him to kiss her.

'Come on, you two,' Jessica urged them from outside. 'I want to see inside.'

Inside, the house was perfectly proportioned, a real family home. It should have radiated warmth and welcome but instead it felt empty . . . cold . . . unlived in . . . its rooms bare and austere.

Lacey was appalled. It was like a hotel. No, it was far, far worse than a hotel. It had a lonely, almost institutionalised air about it, a lack of warmth, of life, of love. There were no pictures, no flowers, no small personal belongings. It was sterile . . . empty.

'How many bedrooms does it have?' she heard Jessica asking Lewis.

'Five,' he responded as he led the way upstairs. 'And three bathrooms.'

A large house for a single man. Why had he bought it?

Upstairs the bedrooms were just as barren of any signs of homeliness as those downstairs. Outside the last door Lewis paused, and then said briefly, 'This last one is my room. I don't think there's any need to show you in there.'

The door was slightly open, and as they walked past a current of air caught it, opening it still further, so that Lacey automatically glanced inside.

On the cabinet beside the bed she could see a silver photograph frame. It was turned towards the bed so that she could not see the photograph inside it, but immediately jealousy tore savagely at her. Now she knew why he hadn't wanted them to see inside his room: it was because he still kept a photograph of her there—the woman he had left her for. His bedroom was obviously still a shrine to her... to his love for her.

As they walked downstairs, Lacey discovered that she was trembling, barely able to contain the intensity of her emotions.

She was a woman, for heaven's sake, not a girl. It was ridiculous, humiliating... idiotic that she should still feel like this

It was bad enough that Lewis was still able to arouse her sexually, but this jealousy... this despair... this aching, yearning envy of another woman because she possessed his love—surely they did not belong to maturity, to wisdom, to common-sense or all the other things she felt went hand in hand with her age?

The kitchen, though large and well-equipped, was as sterile as the rest of the house. While Lewis made them tea, Lacey tried to exercise her imagination by exchanging the streamlined formica units for something a little less severe and more homely, wooden perhaps with tiled worktops; an Aga replacing the modern split-level cooker; gentle, worn tiles on the floor, covered perhaps by a couple of rugs; a chair in front of the Aga; a large scrubbed table in the middle of the room, so that the whole family could . . .

She tensed abruptly. What family? she demanded bitterly of herself. The family Lewis had told her he would never have? This was, after all, Lewis's home and not hers.

And what about her, the other woman? Had she left him when he had told her that he did not intend to have any children? Had he told Lacey that, how would she have reacted? She had always wanted a family—three, hopefully four children. Had Lewis told her in the early days of their marriage that that would not be possible, what would she have done?

Would she have left him to find a man who shared her dream of a family . . . a man who could give her healthy children? Or would her love for Lewis have been more important to her? Would it have kept her by his side ... would she have been prepared to give up her desire to have a family to stay with him? Would her love have been strong enough for that?

She gave a tiny shiver. She thought she knew the answer, but then when she looked at her daughter she wondered ... chewing on her bottom lip, worrying at it, as she wondered if over the years her self-denial might not have become corrosive and bitter, eating into the fabric of her love.

Perhaps it was just as well she had never had to make that choice ... that Lewis had in effect made it for her, by rejecting her before either of them knew the truth.

'You're very quiet.'

Lacey tensed at the soft sound of Lewis's voice. She hadn't even realised he was watching her, and she flushed uncomfortably, wondering how long he had been studying her and what he might have read in her unguarded face.

Even now she found it difficult to appear composed when he focused his attention on her, terrified of what she might inadvertently betray.

It was bad enough that sexually he knew how vulnerable she was to him; if he should discover that she loved him as well ...

She gave a tiny shiver. Even now, days later, she still woke up in the night, vividly aware of how she had felt when he touched her, aching for him ...

wanting him, and acutely, bitterly conscious of the fact that she had practically encouraged, if not invited him to make love to her, but making that idiotic admission that there had been no one else since him.

'She's probably redecorating everywhere,' Jessica told him mischievously, adding, 'Which room have you chosen for the nursery, Ma?'

'The house does need a woman's touch,' Lewis commented, ignoring the latter part of Jessica's comment. 'After I bought it, I . . .' He stopped. 'You still haven't seen the gardens, and we won't want to leave it too late getting back. I've booked a table for us at eight.'

Since it was Jessica's last evening at home, Lewis had insisted on taking them out to dinner. Lacey had protested that there was no need, but Jessica had overruled her, assuring her that she would enjoy the treat.

The gardens were well laid out, mainly lawned, with flower beds which were a little too formal for Lacey's personal taste, although she loved the maturity of the large trees which framed the garden and protected it from view.

While Lewis and Jessica discussed the plausibility of dredging the weed-covered pond and re-stocking it with koi carp, she walked across the lawn towards the small summer-house at the other side of the garden.

The wisteria which grew over it had finished flowering, but the rose entwined with it had a profusion of pink buds, some of them half-open, the sweet scent surrounding her.

'Lacey, are you feeling all right?'

She hadn't heard Lewis approach and she swung round, her face shadowed and pale, her eyes unwittingly revealing the strain she was under.

'Of course I'm not all right,' she told him shortly. 'How could I be? This whole charade... and we don't seem to be any closer to telling Jessica. Where is she, by the way?'

'She thought she saw a fish in the pond. She's still over there looking for it. What would you have preferred? That we told her that we'd simply gone to bed together for old times' sake?' He sounded grimly bitter. 'Is that really the kind of example you want to set her... the impression you want to give her of our relationship?'

'What relationship? We don't *have* a relationship.'

'We did once,' Lewis told her. 'I thought of you when I bought this house. It was so like the one you said you wanted.'

She went white with the shock of it, the looked-for cruelty of his casual comment turning her head away with a quick defensive movement that caused her hair to slide silkily across her face, tears blurring her eyes so that she had to blink furiously to stop them from falling.

'Lacey, what is it...what...?'

He was standing far too close to her, bending towards her, his hand resting on the wall of the summer-house, so that she was virtually imprisoned between it and him.

'Look, I know how much of a strain this whole thing is for you...for both of us...but for Jessica's sake... She's going back to university tomorrow. I do understand how you must feel about the whole thing...but if——'

'But if what?' she demanded raggedly, interrupting him. 'If I hadn't practically begged you to go to bed with me none of this would ever have happened. Do you think I don't know that——?'

'That wasn't actually what I was going to say.' His quiet words cut through her own nervously angry outburst. 'And as for begging me... Look at me, Lacey.'

She darted him a quick glance, her heart suddenly starting to beat far too fast.

'The way I remember it, it wasn't...'

He was standing far far too close to her. She felt dizzy from her awareness of him, from her wretched over-responsiveness to him, and it galled her that even now she seemed completely unable to control her body's physical compulsion for intimacy with him. She could feel herself edging closer to him, feel the soft melting sensation within her, urging her to turn towards him, to...

She must have moved, she realised with sickening disbelief, because suddenly there was no distance between them at all, and the hand which Lewis had been resting against the wall behind her was now touching her shoulder, turning her, holding her.

'Lacey.'

As he whispered her name the warmth of his breath feathered across her mouth, so that immediately her lips softened and parted, her throat tight with tension and need.

As his mouth settled gently on hers she closed her eyes, her whole body melting yearningly into his, her arms wrapping round him as he drew her closer to him.

He kissed her slowly and lingeringly as though he were savouring the taste and feel of her, his lips caressing hers as though his only purpose in life was to cherish and pleasure her.

She tried to resist, to remind herself that in return for this pleasure now she would pay over and over again in time to come in terms of anguish and loss, but her senses were too overwhelmed to listen to reason.

Beneath his mouth she made a soft little sound of appreciation and need, and immediately he responded to it, his arms tightening around her, his body hardening with arousal, his tongue probing the warm depths of her mouth as she clung to him, holding him, wanting him, her breasts aching for the touch of his hands, her body——

'Hey, come on, break it up, you two!'

Lacey wasn't sure which of them was the more shocked by the sound of Jessica's laughter, but when she tried to pull away from him Lewis held on to her, and muttered in her ear, 'No, not yet. I can't.'

She was starting to tremble as reaction set in, but the urgency in his voice made her look at him.

His eyes were very dark, the pupils huge and almost black. There was a thin film of colour under his skin, sharpening the angle of his cheekbones. She could feel the tension in his muscles.

'Just stand here for a minute until...'

Lacey frowned, confused by the blend of irritation and wryness in his voice until he explained bluntly, 'I'm still aroused, Lacey, and, while Jessica obviously knows that we are lovers, I'm still old-fashioned enough to feel a little uncomfortable as her father, for her...'

He broke off as Lacey started to blush, a small smile touching his mouth. He lifted his hand to her face, his fingertips cool against her hot skin.

'So you can still do that. Amazing. Do you remember the first time we made love? How you refused to look at me, and how embarrassed you were when . . . ?'

'I really think the sooner you two set a date and get married the better,' Jessica told them both mock severely as she reached them. 'You're right, Dad,' she added to Lewis. 'It wasn't a fish after all . . .'

Lewis was still standing next to Lacey one arm draped casually around her shoulders, her body turned in towards his own. After what he had said to her, she did not dare to move away; her embarrassment would be even greater than his if he was still as obviously aroused as he had indicated.

A tiny *frisson* of sensation coiled through her, a sweet ache of mingled pride and loss that she could actually have that kind of effect on him.

Don't be ridiculous, she chided herself bitingly. It's a physical reaction to sexual stimulation, that's all. Any woman could have done it. It means nothing in any personal sense . . . nothing at all.

It was almost ten minutes before Lewis let her go, and even then, as the three of them walked back to the house together, he kept her by his side, his arm still around her shoulders. No doubt such pretend intimacy was for Jessica's benefit, but, since they had already agreed that the sooner they could start to intimate to Jessica that things were not after all working out between them the better, it seemed illogical of him to be promoting this image of intimacy between them.

The afternoon had tired her. She told herself as Lewis drove them back home that it was the effect of the fresh air that was making her feel so drained and sleepy, but she knew in reality that it was the emotional strain that was exhausting her, draining her to the point where she felt that all she wanted to do was to go to bed and stay there, waking up only when it was all over and her life was back to normal. When Lewis had disappeared from it.

But if that was what she really wanted, why did the mere thought of a life without him make her feel so miserably bleak and full of despair?

She had got over loving and losing him once, she reminded herself grittily later on when she was changing for the evening. She would get over it again. Or would she? She had been younger then, stronger...with a very definite purpose in life. She had had to think of Jessica, her child. She still had to think of Jessica, of course, but not in the same way. Jessica was an adult herself now.

Her small house only had two bedrooms, fortunately, so Lewis was staying at a local hotel instead of driving home after their meal. Jessica had teased them both about it, remarking that, since she had already caught them in bed to-

gether, there seemed little point in Lewis's returning to his hotel.

'I'm going to miss you both once I'm back at
university,' Jessica commented as she walked into
Lacey's bedroom. 'Still, it won't be long. We'll all
be together again at half-term, and Ian has
arranged for me to have my tests then as
well...which reminds me, I must ring him and
check on exactly when my appointment is.' Her
face shadowed a little. 'I was thinking only the
other night how lucky I am. Not just in being
born, but in living now, when I will have a choice,
when I don't have to make the kind of decision
Dad had to face. I was wondering, Ma. The other
woman...the one he left you for——'

'Jess...please, I don't want to discuss it.' Her
hand shook as she tried to fasten her earring.
'Jess, don't get too...too excited about the
thought of Lewis and me getting back together. I
mean, it's early days yet...it may not...it may not
work out.'

'What?' Jessica stared at her and then laughed.
'Don't be an idiot, Ma. It's plain to see that the
pair of you are madly in love. The way Dad looks
at you when he thinks no one can see him reminds
me of a hungry dog eyeing up a very, very delec-
table bone.'

'Thanks a lot,' Lacey responded drily, dipping her head so that Jessica couldn't see the betraying emotion in her eyes.

Lewis was an excellent actor, she had to give him that, but she wasn't sure that his acting was doing either of them any good. Sooner or later Jessica would have to know the truth. But not until after they knew the results of her tests. As Lewis had pointed out, she would need them both then, especially if the tests proved positive.

'Why don't you go back with Dad tomorrow when he goes home?' Jessica suggested. 'After all, there's nothing to stop you, is there?'

'No? I *do* have a job, remember.'

'Yes, but you'll be giving that up once the two of you remarry, won't you?' Jessica told her confidently. 'I know you'll want to continue with your fund-raising work, and, from what Dad's been saying to me about his involvement in the research into the effects of the disorder, he'll more than support you in that, but if you do have a baby... or two...'

Sighing to herself, Lacey stood up.

'We'd better go downstairs,' she told her daughter. 'Lewis will be here soon.'

CHAPTER EIGHT

THEY were having dinner at the same restaurant where Lacey had taken Jessica on the night of the presentation.

Then she had looked up and across the restaurant, had suffered the shock of seeing Lewis, and hadn't dreamed then for one moment that there would ever come a time when she might be seated opposite him at a table in that same restaurant; she had certainly not envisaged that Jessica would be with them, nor that she would be trapped in a situation where she had to pretend that she and Lewis were considering remarrying.

She had as little appetite now as she had had then, and for the same reason, although now Lewis was sitting a lot closer to her than he had been on that occasion.

To an outsider, no doubt, they presented a picture of happy family intimacy, a close-knit, loving family unit. She closed her eyes against the pain of her own thoughts. Only she knew how much she wished that picture was a true one.

'Are you OK, Ma?' Jessica asked her anxiously. 'You've gone very pale.'

'I'm just tired, that's all,' Lacey fibbed, forcing her mouth into an unwilling smile. For Jessica's sake she had to go along with this charade, at least until they had the results of her tests.

She shook her head when Lewis asked her if she had any preference as regarded their wine, absently noticing that Jessica leaned over to him and whispered something to him as he was beckoning the wine waiter.

Later, when they brought the ice bucket and champagne to the table, she looked at it in bewilderment.

'Jessica's idea,' Lewis explained briefly. 'She thought we ought to celebrate our reconciliation, and to toast the future.'

Once Lacey had loved champagne, enjoying its ice-cold taste on her tongue and the excitement of the bubbles as they slid down her throat; now it made her feel slightly queasy, just as did the food in front of her.

She tried to make an effort, to appear happy and relaxed, but she knew from the brief looks that Lewis occasionally gave her that, although she might have deceived Jessica, she had not deceived him.

It caused an odd weakening sensation in the pit of her stomach to realise that it was not her daughter who knew her the best, who had registered her real feelings, but Lewis.

It was a relief when the evening finally drew to a close and they left the restaurant.

In the comfort of Lewis's car, with the tyres swishing soothingly on the tarmac, she found her eyes closing and her body growing heavy with sleep, and several times during the short journey she discovered that she was having to force herself to stay awake.

When Lewis brought the car to a standstill outside the house she fumbled automatically for the door-handle, tensing when he reached across her to open the door for her, drawing her body back into her seat to avoid coming into contact with him.

She saw from the look he gave her that he recognised what she was doing, although she couldn't understand why her action should make him look so bitterly angry. Jessica wasn't watching them. She was already out of the car.

'You look exhausted,' he told her flatly and unflatteringly. 'I shan't stay. I'll see you in, but I shan't stay.'

Jessica, though, had other ideas. As the three of them walked towards the house she announced blithely, 'Now I intend to have an early night, so you two needn't worry about my playing gooseberry. To judge from that kiss I witnessed this afternoon, you'd both appreciate some time on your own.'

Lacey stumbled on the path, and instantly Lewis reached out to steady her. The last thing she could handle right now was time alone with him, and yet if she objected . . . protested, Jessica was going to start asking questions.

Once they were inside and Jessica had said her goodnights, Lewis said quietly to her. 'I'm sorry about this. Look, why don't you go and sit down? I'll make us both a cup of tea.'

It was only as she nodded her head and opened the kitchen door that she realised that this was her house, and that she should be the one playing host, instead of allowing Lewis to take charge.

And yet, instead of feeling resentment or irritation, it was almost a relief to open the sitting-room door and to slip off her shoes and curl up on the settee.

She was asleep when Lewis came back in with the tea-tray. He studied her broodingly for a time. This afternoon in his arms she had felt so . . . so *right,* as though she belonged there; as though she *wanted* to belong there, and then he had kissed her and she had aroused him so damn much. He put down the tea-tray quietly so as not to disturb her, and then walked over to her.

'Lacey.'

The sound of Lewis's voice brought Lacey out of her sleep. She blinked in confusion as she looked up at him, realising that he must have switched off the light when he came into the room because now it was only illuminated by the soft glow of a table-lamp.

'I'm sorry to wake you, but if you stay curled up like that for much longer you'll get cramp. I've made some tea.'

Lacey looked towards the tray on the coffee-table. She felt disorientated, tired, as though she had been asleep for much longer than a few minutes.

She struggled to sit up and put her feet down on the floor but, as she moved, Lewis's prediction came true and agonising cramp shot through her leg.

She cried out automatically, reaching towards her calf, but Lewis beat her to it, his fingers curling firmly round her skin, massaging the cramped muscles.

Almost immediately the pain started to recede, relaxing its grip on her body.

'It's...it's gone now,' she told Lewis huskily, drawing herself away from him and trying to sit upright.

He had been leaning towards her while he massaged her leg, but now as he released her he sat down beside her on the settee, his body far too close to her own.

Had she thought about it she would have chosen one of the chairs to sit in, but it had never occurred to her that she might get cramp, nor that he would actually choose to sit beside her. Perhaps he was thinking of Jessica, she reflected painfully, although it was highly unlikely that their daughter would come downstairs, not after what she had said to them before going to bed.

'It's rather like being two teenagers again, knowing someone is upstairs, listening,' Lewis commented ruefully as he reached across her to pour the tea. 'Only in our case it's not being caught out doing something we shouldn't that's the problem, but being caught out *not* doing something we *should*.'

'I don't think Jess will come down,' Lacey told him, unable to stop her glance from straying to the clock on the video.

'It's too soon,' Lewis told her, reading her mind. 'I know we're supposed to be impatient and in love, but I think that, no matter how impatiently I might be supposed to have made love to you, Jess would consider it less than romantic of me to leave so quickly. After all, as far as she's concerned we have plans to make...a future to discuss.'

Lacey bent her head so that he wouldn't see the emotion in her eyes. When he talked of their being lovers ... of their having a future, no matter how hard she fought against it, she couldn't help being emotionally affected by the difference between the fiction and the reality.

Already, after so short a space of time, she had grown so dependent on his being there, on being able to see him ... talk with him ... so that, no matter how much pain his pretence caused her, once he was gone what she would have to endure would be even worse.

To try to distract herself and keep her mind off her emotional vulnerability, she said unsteadily, 'It must have been very difficult for you when you discovered ... when you learned about ... about the disorder, especially since, like Jessica, you had had no idea when you were growing up.'

She looked across at him and saw the emotion flicker through his eyes.

'Difficult. Yes, I suppose it was, although at the time there was almost too much to do ... too many other things to think about. I didn't really have time to dwell on it or ...'

He stopped abruptly. His voice had been clipped, his words terse as though even speaking about the subject at all was something he would have preferred not to do.

Realising that he had most probably only discovered the truth at about the the time he had divorced her and was living with his new love, Lacey could well understand what he meant, although it still must have come as a terrible shock, to him and to the woman he loved.

She tried to imagine how she would have felt had he still been married to her when he made the discovery. How would she have reacted? How had that other woman reacted?

Not wanting to probe, and yet feeling that she had to ask, she enquired softly, 'How *did* you find out, Lewis? You told me that you didn't know about the inherited tendency when you and I married and . . .'

'It was my father. He told me. Or, rather, he wrote to me.'

Lacey stared at him. 'Your *father*?'

'Yes. Remember how you encouraged me to contact him by making enquiries through Australia House? When eventually the authorities there managed to trace him, I wrote to him explaining who I was, telling him that Mother had died, telling him that I was m . . . that I would like to make contact with him.

'Quite some time went by without any response, and then one day there was a letter. Not the letter I had hoped for,' he told her bleakly.

'In it, he, my father, told me that the reason, or one of the reasons, he had left my mother was because he had discovered that she was a carrier. Apparently *she* had known but had kept it a secret from him. When I was born there were complications, various tests had to be carried out, and the truth came to light.

'My parents were told then that if I had inherited the disorder then the chances were that I wouldn't survive beyond my early teens.

'My father was one of those men who wanted sons. A very macho man... in that sense. I would say a complete coward in others. He obviously couldn't face up to what had happened, and so he left my mother... divorced her and went to live in Australia.

'She never told me any of this, and by some fluke I turned out to be one of the rare cases where, although I had inherited the defective gene, the effects of the disorder had never materialised.

'When I received that letter—at first I couldn't believe it... didn't want to believe it. It was like a nightmare... like descending into hell. I had no idea who to turn to... what to do. There I was, m...'

He paused. 'Perhaps in my own way I was as much a coward as my father. All I know is I couldn't bear the thought of putting any woman through what my mother must have had to endure with me . . . what, I had now learned, women carrying the disorder did go through when they gave birth to male children, and so . . .'

'So you opted for a vasectomy,' Lacey supplied for him.

For a moment he hesitated. His face was pale and set, a muscle jerking painfully in his jaw.

'Yes. I opted for a vasectomy,' he agreed heavily.

Lacey had no idea what to say. She was overwhelmed with shock and compassion. How could any father treat his son the way Lewis's had treated him? She could hardly bear to remember that she had been the one who had initially encouraged him to seek him out.

'If I hadn't encouraged you to find your father . . .' she began painfully, but he shook his head, stopping her.

'No, you mustn't say that. Far, far better that I did find out than . . .' He stopped and swallowed and Lacey knew he must be thinking of *her* . . . that other woman. Where was she now? Why had they split up? Had it been because of his disorder?

Impulsively she reached out towards him, placing her hand on his arm. Beneath her fingertips his flesh felt hot, the muscles hard. The sensation of his skin beneath her own momentarily distracted her, and then she looked up at him and saw the bleakness in his eyes and told him softly, 'Lewis,

I'm so sorry. I don't know what happened...between you...you and her, but no woman who loved...who loved a man could ever turn away from him because he...because he had made the decision not to have any children...no matter how much she herself might have wanted them.'

As she spoke she knew illuminatingly that for her it was true, that, given the choice all those years ago, even though she had desperately wanted a family, she would willingly have sacrificed that need to be with him. Lewis himself would always have had prior claim on her love.

'No. Maybe not...but I could never live with myself if I had asked a woman, especially a woman whom I knew wanted children, to give them up...no matter how much she might love me. To do so would have been cheating on her and cheating on our love.'

He was looking at her as he spoke, and for some reason his words made her ache and tremble almost as though they were directed at her, and not towards someone else.

'You're a very compassionate woman, Lacey,' he told her rawly. 'The kind of woman it's all too dangerously easy for a man to love.'

And then he raised his hands to her face and, gently cupping it, leaned forward and kissed her mouth.

It was, she recognised as tears stung her eyes, a kiss of peace... of sadness... a kiss without passion or need; and yet, even as the thought formed, it changed, the pressure of his mouth hardening fractionally, the way his hands held her face betraying a hint of tension.

Almost without knowing what she was doing, she moved towards him, her mouth soft and inviting, her lips clinging to his.

For a moment she thought that it was going to happen, that he was after all going to kiss her, and then outside an owl hooted and he was releasing her, moving away from her, saying unsteadily, 'I'd better go. It's getting late.'

'You'll call round in the morning to see Jessica off,' Lacey reminded him as she too stood up.

In the half-darkness he hesitated, almost as though he was torn between leaving and coming back to her. She held her breath, waiting... hoping... and then didn't know whether to be disappointed or relieved when he finally turned back to the door, confirming, 'Yes, I'll be here.'

'So that's it now, until half-term,' Jessica mourned as she put the last of her things in her car. 'Still, never mind, it isn't long to wait, and once we get these tests out of the way... Well, let's just say that I'm rather looking forward to having two parents to come home to.'

Guilt, pain, and illogically something close to anger followed one another in quick succession as Lacey listened to her daughter.

The anger she suppressed. It was unfair of her to feel resentful and hurt, to feel almost as though she had to justify herself and her actions to Jessica. After all, it wasn't Jessica's fault that she had found Lewis and her mother in bed together, was it?

But sooner or later Jessica would have to be told the truth, and Lacey was beginning to wish that she had been told it right from the start.

Lewis had already left. He had called round earlier on to wish Jessica a safe journey and then had announced that he had to leave.

To Lacey he had said quietly that he knew she would want a few minutes to herself with Jessica. His consideration had surprised her a little, bringing the quick sting of emotional tears to her eyes.

She had become far *too* emotional recently, *too* quick to allow her feelings to control her life, her nerves in a constant state of rawness and tension.

She had wanted Lewis to go, had been relieved to see him go; and yet at the same time she had longed for him to stay, for him...for him to what? To love her as she had once believed that he did? Was she really so stupid?

The trouble was that these last few days, with their too evocative intimacy with him, their pseudo-closeness, had confused her brain to the point where even it was sometimes in danger of believing in the fiction they had created. When Lewis stood next to her, when he touched her, when he looked at her, her need to respond to him was so intense that she could barely control it.

Now he had gone, and just as soon as Jessica had had her tests done and the results were known, just as soon as they were sure that she was over the trauma of them, they would be able to start convincing her that they were not, after all, planning to get back together.

But in the meantime...

In the meantime she had work to do, she reminded herself as she gave Jessica a last warm kiss and then waved her off.

She had already warned Tony Aimes that she would be late getting into the office.

When she did arrive he greeted her warmly, giving her an affectionate hug.

Why was it, she wondered dispassionately as she disengaged herself, that the embrace of one man should leave her emotions and her flesh so cold, while the merest touch of another...?

From the comments Tony made to her as she worked, she guessed that he had heard something about Lewis, although he didn't ask her outright who he was, or what role he had in her life.

Lacey responded vaguely to his discreet probing, telling herself uncomfortably that, since Lewis did not and could not have any real or permanent role in her life, it was pointless discussing with anyone the close relationship they had once shared.

She worked late, dealing with a query from abroad which had cropped up at the last minute, and then drove home, feeling edgy and tense.

At the back of her mind, unwanted and dangerous, lay the knowledge that she was half hoping that, even though with Jessica back at university there was no real reason for him to do so, Lewis would get in touch with her. Half hoping . . . and half dreading.

When the evening passed without the telephone ringing once, she told herself that she was glad, that it was a relief to her that Lewis had not tried to get in touch, and yet when she went to bed she was thinking about him, wondering what he was doing and who he was with.

Although it had been obvious from his conversation that his business had done extremely well and that he had a close-knit group of friends, there had never been any reference by him to anyone special . . . a woman . . . *the* woman.

But then, he was hardly likely to do so, was he?

A week slipped by, her days almost too busy as she caught up with the work which had piled up during her absence, but despite her tiredness she wasn't sleeping very well, her thoughts constantly returning to Lewis.

It was the strain of the fiction she had been forced to live under while Jessica was at home, she told herself unsteadily as she fought to banish the mental images of Lewis which continued to crowd her mind, threatening to take over her whole life.

On Friday evening, just as she was walking into the house, the phone started to ring. She raced to pick up the receiver, her heart pounding, her stomach clenching on an agony of apprehension and tension, but it was only Ian, ringing to confirm the arrangements for Jessica's tests.

'By the way,' he added rather stiltedly, 'I understand that congratulations are in order.' When Lacey said nothing, he continued uncomfortably, 'Jessica has told me your good news. I must say that it came as something of a shock. I had no idea that Lewis and you... Of course I'm delighted for both of you, and Jessica obviously is over the moon. I understand you haven't set an actual date yet, but——'

'Jessica told you that Lewis and I are getting married?' Lacey interrupted him huskily.

'Yes. Yes, that's right. I do understand that it isn't common knowledge yet. I must say that

Lewis is a very lucky man, Lacey. I'm very happy for you, my dear. For both of you ... but most especially for you, even though ...'

He continued to talk for several more minutes while Lacey closed her eyes, thankful that there was no one with her to witness the shock his disclosures had given her.

How could Jessica have done this to her? How could she have intimated to Ian that she and Lewis ...?

Numbly she replaced the receiver, her first impulse to ring Jessica and demand to know what on earth she had thought she was doing dying as she realised how futile such an action would be.

What on earth was she going to do now? Ian wasn't a gossip, and he was a close friend, but even so ... Her stomach muscles clenched in an agony of mortification as she thought of the gossip which would ensue once people knew that she and Lewis were not going to remarry.

It was all very well at Jessica's age to shake off as unimportant the views and comments of others. And as for Lewis ... well, this wasn't *his* home. He wouldn't have to live with the consequences of any gossip, while she ...

There was only one thing for it: she would have to go and see Lewis to tell him what had happened and see if there was some way of repairing the damage Jessica had unwittingly done. After all, surely he would want people assuming that the two of them were going to get married as little as she did herself?

She was still wearing her office clothes. It was a warm fine evening and before setting out she went upstairs, showered and changed into a pair of jeans and a soft T-shirt.

Without her high heels she looked almost too small to be adult, and wasn't it perhaps time she opted for a more sophisticated and mature hairstyle than her shoulder-length bob, something that would give her more authority and maturity?

Grimacing at herself in the mirror, she went back downstairs, collected her keys and her shoulder-bag, and let herself out of the house.

It was only when she had driven over halfway to Lewis's that she allowed herself to admit that she could probably more easily have discussed what had happened with him over the telephone.

Some things had to be said face to face, she told herself defensively, ignoring the tiny inner voice that taunted her that she was just using Ian's phone call as an excuse to go running after Lewis ... that it wasn't so much her shock at discovering that Ian believed they were getting married that was motivating her, but her longing to see Lewis ... to be with him.

Guiltily trying to banish such potentially disruptive thoughts, she concentrated on her driving.

It was a beautiful early summer evening, the countryside lush and green. Envy and nostalgia ached inside her as she passed a young couple walking together hand in hand, gazing into one another's eyes, their love for one another so plain, so obvious that it brought a lump to her throat.

Once she and Lewis had been like that. Once...

When she arrived at the house and turned into the drive, without Lewis's presence and its effect on her to distract her, she was acutely conscious of the house's air of forlorness.

Lewis and his home both shared an aloneness, she recognised as she parked her car and got out.

When she knocked on the door there was no reply, and neither was there any sign of Lewis's car. See what you get for behaving so impetuously and stupidly? she derided herself. You come rushing over here, totally unnecessarily, and it serves you right that Lewis isn't in.

And yet, instead of getting straight back in her car, turning it round and driving home, she wandered round the side of the house and into the rear garden, reluctant to listen to the voice of common sense and restraint, wanting rather to stay where she was as though in some way being here in Lewis's home brought her closer to him.

Fool, she told herself as she walked across the lawn, but her emotions, her senses refused to respond to her taunts.

Lewis. How stupid it was of her to still love him like this... yearning for him, aching for him as though her physical and emotional growth had been halted when he had left her, as though she were still that same girl who had thought he loved her as deeply and permanently as she loved him.

The roses cloaking the summer-house blurred and trembled, but it wasn't until she blinked that Lacey realised it was because she had started to cry.

Why, after nearly twenty years of firmly controlling her emotions, was she now behaving like this—bursting into tears without warning, suffering all the emotional upheaval and agony of a woman deeply in love?

Perhaps because she *was* a woman deeply in love. A woman hopelessly in love.

She covered her face with her hands, weeping silently, her body convulsing as she gave in to the deep welling tide of emotion destroying her self-control.

Lewis. She loved him so much.

Somewhere in the distance she heard the sound of a car, but the noise barely registered, unable to penetrate the intensity of her grief.

Lewis. Too late now to wish that fate had never seen fit to bring him back into her life. Into Jessica's life.

The first thing Lewis had seen when he turned into his drive was Lacey's car, and as he parked his own and unfastened his seatbelt his face was creased with sharp anxiety.

Something was wrong. Something *had* to be wrong to bring Lacey here to see him.

His heart started to pound, fear twisting his guts. It was Jessica. Something had happened. The tests.

As he rounded the corner of the house and saw Lacey standing motionless with her back to him, his fears were confirmed.

As he sprinted across the lawn towards her, calling her name, she turned her head.

In the sunlight he could see quite clearly the traces of her tears, and the pain in her eyes.

Without even thinking about what he was doing, he caught hold of her, holding her, cradling her against him, his hand in her hair, stroking it, smoothing it, while his own body was trembling almost as much as hers.

'Lacey. Don't...please don't. Don't cry, my darling. Just tell me what's wrong...Jessica...it's Jessica, isn't it...?'

CHAPTER NINE

JESSICA!

Lacey tensed, lifting her head from Lewis's chest.

The shock of seeing him racing towards her across the lawn, and then taking hold of her, cradling her, whispering her name, stroking her hair, treating her with such tenderness and concern, coming so unexpectedly on top of her bleak thoughts had left her with no defences to withstand him, but now suddenly she was shocked back to reality.

She could hear the anguish in his voice, and, knowing it was for their daughter, she was torn between her instinctive need to reassure him that nothing was wrong, and the shocking awareness of her jealousy of her daughter, that she should be the one to arouse him to such concern... such emotion.

She trembled in his arms, disgusted by her own emotions. How could she resent the fact that he loved Jessica?

As he felt her tremble, the pressure of his arm around her tightened. She heard him give a small groan and felt the deep shuddering breath he took.

'Lacey... darling. Look at me. Tell me.'

Darling... he had called her darling. Confusion swirled through her, lifting her head from his chest so that she could focus on him.

'It isn't Jessica,' she managed to tell him huskily. 'She's... she's fine.'

'Not Jessica?' He was frowning now, and she tensed, waiting for him to release her, to step back from her, to repudiate and reject her; but, although the pressure of his arm relaxed a little as the tension left him, it still stayed firmly round her, and the hand which had been in her hair now cradled the back of her neck, his fingers stroking her tense muscles. 'Then what...?'

He was looking at her... searching her eyes so intently that she had to look away, unable to sustain the scrutiny. His glance dropped to her mouth, and lingered there. She was as acutely conscious of it as though he had actually touched her.

The tender flesh of her lips burned and felt so unbearably dry that she just had to moisten them, just had to open her mouth and touch the burning dry heat of her lips with her tongue tip.

'Lacey.' The harsh protest shocked her into looking directly at him. 'You've been crying.' His fingertips touched her face, tracing the path of her tears. 'What is it? What's wrong?'

She shook her head, unable to answer, just as a large fat bumble bee flew dozily towards her. As she ducked her head to avoid it, her hair swung against Lewis's skin. He raised his hand, his fingers entangling in its silkiness, and then as she looked at him, her eyes round and startled, he said her name in a low jerky voice and bent his head towards her.

Mesmerised, she waited, unable to withdraw her body from within the circle of his arm, nor her gaze from his mouth.

Only when it finally touched her own did she close her eyes, her whole body trembling with aching anticipation.

His hand touched her face, cupping it gently, his fingers skimming her skin before sliding into her hair, supporting the weight of her head while he kissed her.

His skin carried the hot musky scent of an active male body, intensifying her own arousal, making her snuggle closer to him, her body pressing against his.

'Lacey.'

The sound he made as he said her name thrilled through her. It needed no translation, no explanation, its message as clear as the one given by the fierce hardening of his body.

She aroused him and he wanted her. Her senses trembled with exultant joy that he should so clearly feel what she herself was experiencing.

'I want you so much,' she heard him whispering shakily to her. 'So very, very much.'

He was still kissing her, and she opened her mouth beneath his, pressing herself closer to him, sliding her hands up under his jacket, her heart beating furiously fast as the tenor of their kiss changed, the slow gentle pressure of Lewis's mouth giving way to something else, something more demanding and emotionally charged.

As she responded to it, welcoming the intimacy, she knew that *she* was responsible for what was happening, that *she* was the one who had subtly encouraged and invited the passion they were now sharing.

Her mind screamed a volley of warnings and objections to her, but her senses screened them out. They weren't what they wanted to hear. What she wanted to hear was the erotic counterplay of Lewis's breathing, the soft sound of his hands as they moved against her body, the delirious control destroying the messages her senses and her emotions were relaying to her.

All around them the garden was full of the rich evening scent of the roses and growing things. The week had been dry, and when Lewis lowered her on to the grass she was conscious of the earth's warmth and the clean green smell of the grass, long where it edged towards the trees and soft against her face as she turned blindly towards Lewis, seeking a renewal of the kiss they had been sharing.

When he hesitated, cupping her face, smoothing his thumbs over her skin, searching her eyes, she read the question he had not yet asked her. Her heart trembled inside her body. There were a hundred—no, a thousand reasons why she shouldn't be doing this, but none of them mattered.

As she reached towards him her hands trembled as they slid up over his arms, free of the restriction of the jacket he had shrugged off.

She watched as his eyes betrayed the effect she was having on him, dizzy with the knowledge that she should be able to call up so much desire from him.

'Common sense tells me that we shouldn't be doing this,' he told her huskily as he leaned over her. 'But right now there's nothing that I want more than to hold you in my arms. Do you remember how it used to be between us?'

Did she . . .? Her eyes grew huge and dark, reflecting his desire. Her hands trembled as she held him.

'So many, many times I've dreamed of holding you like this.'

He was leaning over her, unfastening the row of tiny buttons fastening her T-shirt, laying her body bare to the evening sun and to the touch of his hands and his lips.

She shuddered wildly, her lips pressed tightly together as she struggled to suppress her emotions. The touch of his lips was so familiar, so...so tender...so...so adoring.

Her hands came up, clasping the back of his head, her body arching in fierce response as his hands cupped her bare breasts and his lips tasted her sun-warmed skin.

'You're so beautiful...so perfect.'

The humble, marvelling tone of his voice made her throat close with emotion, the sight of his dark head against her breast heart-stoppingly poignant. She was a woman now, not a girl, and for twenty years she had scarcely given her body a thought in the sexual sense, and yet now, suddenly, she found she was afraid almost, conscious of the difference physically between a woman of twenty and a woman of thirty-eight. But Lewis's body had changed as well, and to her eyes for the better.

He kissed the hollow between her breasts, his tongue stroking her skin, and then the slope of her breast itself, his kisses delicate, gentle as though he was afraid of hurting her.

When he withdrew from her, carefully covering her exposed breasts with her T-shirt, her feelings must have shown in her eyes because suddenly his own changed, darkening, glittering almost, his voice rough as he told her, 'It isn't that I don't want to. It's just that I'm afraid...afraid that once I have you in my mouth, that once I...I'm afraid of losing my self-control...of hurting you...rushing you. I've dreamed of this for such a long, long time...wanted you...ached for you——' He saw that she was crying and stopped, demanding abruptly, 'What is it...what have I said? If you want me to stop...'

Logic told her that that was exactly what she should say she *did* want, but she refused to listen. He was sitting up now, watching her anxiously, his eyes shadowed, his body tense.

She sat up too, shaking her head, knowing that there was no way she could say to him what was in her heart, no way she could simply tell him how much she loved and wanted him...no way she dared risk spoiling the magical wonder of what was happening with clumsy explanations and questions.

She wasn't a girl any longer, ruled by the expectations of an outside society. She was a woman, and free to make her own decisions. Giving in to her love for Lewis now, showing him how much she wanted and needed him would hurt . . . need concern no one other than herself.

Before she could lose her courage she reached for him, her fingers trembling as she unfastened the buttons on his shirt.

For a moment he didn't move, but then when he realised what she was doing he started to help her, wrenching the shirt off with the cuff buttons still fastened so that he had to yank hard on the sleeves, causing the cuff buttons to fly off, making Lacey laugh, her laughter half nervous tension, half shock at the sensation that shot through her stomach at the sight of his bare torso.

It was ridiculous that the sight of a man's bare chest should affect her like this, making her hands tremble as she touched him, causing her to . . .

She touched his throat with her lips, hesitantly at first, her touch uncertain as she tensed herself against his physical reaction.

A vein throbbed in his neck. She touched it with her fingertips, measuring the furious race of his pulse. Beneath her other hand his body hair felt warm and damp, his nipple a hard point against her palm. Slowly her kisses became less hesitant, more certain, more eager.

She heard him moan, the sound thrilling her; felt the warmth of his hands against her bare back, felt the deliciously wanton friction of his body hair against her breasts as he gathered her against him, his lips against her ear as he warned her shakily, 'Lacey, don't. Please don't do this, unless you mean it, unless you want me as much as I want you.'

Reluctantly she lifted her lips from his throat, her eyes slumbrous, her expression soft with love and need.

'Isn't it obvious that I . . . that I want you?' she asked him tremulously, looking down at their bodies, at the taut erect points of her nipples.

His gaze followed hers. She felt him catch his breath and saw the deep flush of colour run up under his skin.

His hands cupped her breasts as he whispered her name, his head dipping down over her body.

At first the warm suckle of his mouth was restrained, controlled, but even so a thousand memories came flooding back, her body responding both to them and to him, her back arching, her fingers digging into his shoulders, a tiny sob of desire muffled in her throat, her body shaking with the emotions inside her.

It broke through his self-control, the sudden hard, urgent pressure of his mouth causing her to whimper softly and cling to him, forbidden words of plea and praise flooding from her as she arched and twisted against him, her senses overwhelmed by the pleasure he was giving her.

Even the fierce rake of his teeth, as his own control was swept away, was a sharply fierce sensual pleasure, an erotic underlining of the completeness of his desire for her.

Her jeans and the rest of his clothes were somehow removed, urgency overtaking finesse, so that the sensation of skin against skin when they were finally free of them was so acutely heightened—for her at least—that Lacey actually felt her response to it deep within her body, a familiar tensing of certain muscles, a familiar awareness that just a kiss, a touch would be enough.

As she tensed Lewis looked at her, tensing too, demanding huskily, 'What is it? If you've changed your mind, if you want to stop...'

She shook her head, unable to speak, instead taking his hand and placing it against her body so that he would know for himself how much she wanted him.

Delicate colour fluctuated under her skin as she did so, and saw the aroused awareness come into his eyes.

Perhaps her younger self might never have done such a thing, might never have been the one to indicate her wants or needs, but she could hardly pretend now that she did not want him, and his own arousal was, after all, obvious for them both to see.

She remembered how once, at first, she had found the sight of his naked body unnerving... not frightening, perhaps, but neither had she felt completely comfortable with his nudity. But now she welcomed the freedom he was giving her to look at him, to watch and touch him and watch him as she did so, her senses measuring his erotic reaction to each caress.

Seeing that he wanted her increased her own desire, her own need, and as she leaned forward to caress him with her lips, to show him how greatly she desired him, she felt again the familiar sharp spasm of sensation within her own body, and shuddered with the force of it.

As she closed her eyes, she heard Lewis saying urgently, 'Lacey... oh, God, Lacey.'

And then he was holding her, touching her, entering her and possessing her so immediately and so powerfully, as though he knew exactly how she had felt, how much she had suddenly needed him there within her, that she cried out, unable to bear the pleasure of it in silence, moving against him, whispering his name, telling him how much she wanted and needed him.

It was a fierce, short-lived coming together, a powerful explosion of sensation that left Lacey feeling weak and dizzy, clinging to Lewis while her body shook with its aftermath.

She could feel Lewis kissing her, holding her; his lips touched her ear, and he told her shakily, 'In all these years there's never been a day, an hour when I haven't wanted you, ached for you ... remembered ... how it was between us; but I realise now that those memories were only pale shadows of reality. Mercifully so, because I could never have endured living with memories of that kind of reality ... of knowing ...'

Lacey opened her eyes and looked at him, her voice full of pain. 'It didn't work out, then, with her—the ... the woman you left me for.'

'What?' He cupped her face, holding her so that she couldn't avoid looking at him. 'What other woman?' he demanded huskily. 'There never was any other woman. I just let you think that because ... because it made it easier ... easier to let you go, to tell myself that I was doing the right thing for you if not for myself ... that you'd find someone else ... someone who could give you children, and that when you did if you'd known the truth you'd have been grateful to me.'

'There *was* no other woman?' Lacey could scarcely take it in. 'But you said. You ...'

Lewis shook his head. 'No, *you* said. I merely said our marriage had to end. I hadn't got as far as thinking of anything so sophisticated as pretending there was someone else. I was still sick with the shock of discovering what I had inherited. All I could think of was that I must not allow you to find out... that your life must not be torn apart and destroyed the way mine had been.'

'No other woman,' Lacey repeated slowly. 'You mean you left me... divorced me because...?'

'Because I'd found out from my father about the gene I was carrying.'

'You divorced me because of *that*? You let me think you no longer wanted me...no longer loved me because of that?'

All her shock...her horror was betrayed by her voice, her eyes huge and accusing as she stared at him. 'Did you really think I was so weak...so...so shallow that knowing the truth would have made any difference at all to me? Didn't you realise how much I loved you?'

His face had gone white. 'Yes, I knew,' he said simply, not trying to evade her. 'But I also knew how much you wanted children. How important a family was to you. Had I known about the hereditary disorder before we married...had I been in a position to grow up knowing about it...to discuss it with you...to be honest with you...but...well, when you married me it was in the belief that we would have children. You'd told me how important that was to you, remember? What right did I have to turn round and tell you that we couldn't have those children?'

'But I loved you... *you*, not some mythical father of children I hadn't even conceived!' Lacey protested vehemently.

'You say that now, but think, Lacey. You were so young. I know you loved me. I know how loyal you are... were. I know you would have stayed with me...and continued to love me...for a while at least, but how long would that love have lasted? A year... two maybe... maybe even longer, but I couldn't live with the fear that one day you would turn away from me... that one day your need for children would outweigh your pity for me. I had to set you free. Free to find someone else.' He heard the sound she made and stopped and then asked her, 'Why didn't you find someone else?'

'You hurt me too much.'

It was cruel and unfair, and she hated herself the moment she had said it, biting her bottom lip and shaking her head.

'No. No, that isn't entirely true, Lewis. You did hurt me...unbearably so. I couldn't believe at first that all the time you had been telling me you loved me there had been someone else. I was afraid to trust another man, to believe that he might love me... and then I had Jessica. She filled my life... my heart, and besides...'

She lifted her head and looked directly at him.

'It's pointless lying about it now. I never stopped loving you. Oh, I tried. I even told myself I'd succeeded, but then I'd dream about you at night and wake up in tears, aching inside from wanting you... loving you. Perhaps if I'd *allowed* myself to forget you there might have been another man.'

'Just as if I had allowed myself to forget about you there might have been another woman. I did contemplate it. A divorcee with a couple of children who didn't want any more. It seemed an ideal solution, but there was also you... and certain memories of the way it had been for us that refused to allow me to want that kind of intimacy with someone who wasn't you.

'I can't give you back all the lost years, Lacey. I can't give you anything now that I couldn't give you twenty years ago, but, if it helps at all, I've never stopped loving you. Never stopped wishing things had been different. Sometimes, God help me, almost wished I had never found my father... never known.'

He gave a deep shudder. Lacey reached out and touched him gently. 'You must have come close to hating me for that. Because if I hadn't suggested you look for him...'

He shook his head. 'I could never hate you, no matter what happened. I hated myself, though... hated myself for still wanting you... for never truly setting you free.'

'If only you had told me... shared it with me.'

'And caused you eventually to turn from me...to hate me the way my father ended up hating my mother...rejecting me...the way he had rejected me?'

Lacey hesitated and then asked him quietly, 'If you had known...about Jessica...would that...?'

'Don't ask me,' Lewis told her. 'Because I don't know the answer. The way I felt then, the panic...the fear...the self-hatred I was experiencing—God help me, but I think I would have wanted you to have a termination.' He saw her face and closed his eyes. 'I'm sorry, Lacey, but I can't lie to you. Not again. I was still too raw from my own discoveries...from knowing that my father had rejected me... All I know is that I would have tried to justify my decision by saying it was to protect you...to protect our marriage...that the risk was too great. Even when I first realised that Jess might be mine, my strongest emotion was one of panic...of fear—fear of both her rejection and yours...of your condemnation of me...fear of the burden of my own guilt because she had been conceived...because I had been careless.'

'I was the one who was careless,' Lacey pointed out wryly.

'You must despise me for what I felt...for the way I reacted. I *did* want Jess to consider being sterilised...but then when she came to see me . . . and I saw her and realised that this was my daughter . . . my child . . . The wonder of it . . . the awe—I can't describe how I felt. It was like stepping out from beneath an immense cloud, the darkness and weight of which had become so much a part of my life that I scarcely even recognised that they were there any longer. I had become so used to being alone . . . to keeping my friends in the dark about the real reason I wasn't married . . . didn't have any family. Suddenly there was someone I could be open with . . . share things with. And suddenly once again there was you.

'I've never stopped loving you, Lacey, and I've no right to ask you this, but could you . . . would you . . . is there any possibility of our starting again . . . marrying again?'

'Only if you promise that never, ever again will you keep anything from me . . . no matter how painful it may be—to either of us.'

It was only when he kissed her that she realised that they were both still naked.

Over an hour later, Lewis protested huskily against her ear, 'If we stay out here much longer the dew will come down and we'll both end up with rheumatism. Why don't we go inside? The house isn't exactly warm and cosy, but at least it does have a large double bed.'

Lazily Lacey gathered up her clothes and put them on, laughing a little when she saw the look in his eyes. 'Think of all the fun you'll have taking them off again later,' she teased him as they walked arm in arm towards the house.

'Really? I thought you were the one who was going to have fun taking mine off,' Lewis teased her back.

The first thing she saw as she walked into the bedroom was the silver photograph frame. She walked to the side of the bed and looked at it, her eyes widening in surprise as she recognised the photograph inside it.

It was one of herself and Jessica.

'I'm sorry. I shouldn't have taken it, but I couldn't resist,' Lewis apologised, coming to stand beside her. 'Forgive me, Lacey.'

As she held him in her arms, Lacey knew it wasn't the theft of the photograph he was asking forgiveness for.

'I forgive you,' she whispered as he kissed her. 'I forgive you, Lewis.'

'Why are you crying?' the small page-boy asked Lacey curiously.

'Because she's Jessica's mother, and mothers always cry at weddings,' one of the older boys told him loftily.

Over their heads, Lewis shot her an amused smile and said softly, 'I must admit, I feel like shedding the odd tear or two myself. Our eldest daughter married . . .'

'Mm. She and Tom are so well-suited, and he says he's thrilled with the idea of being the head of an all-female family. No competition from any other men, or so he claims, and a bevy of beautiful women to spoil him.'

'Mm. Well, I don't want to disillusion him, but when I see what a pair of tomboys our two youngest have turned out to be . . .'

Lacey laughed.

'Well, they don't look like tomboys today,' she pointed out, glancing over to where their twin daughters were standing with the other bridesmaids, their blonde hair caught up with flowers, their peach dresses emphasising the soft purity of their six-year-old complexions.

'Looks can be deceptive,' Lewis said wryly. 'I caught the pair of them daring the page-boy to climb up that oak tree over there ten minutes ago.'

Lacey laughed, leaning her head against him and watching him lovingly.

It had taken a good deal of persuasion before he had agreed to have his vasectomy reversed, and then had come all the trauma and problems of the in vitro fertilisation process which would ensure that only eggs resulting in the birth of female children were returned to her womb.

The decision to opt to have twins had been a joint one, neither of them wanting a solitary child who might feel isolated in having older parents, and it was a decision neither of them had ever regretted, no matter how exhausting the twins could be at times.

In the early days of their marriage the realisation that Jessica had inherited his flawed gene had weighed very heavily on Lewis, more heavily on him than it had done on Jessica herself, Lacey recognised, but then two years ago Jessica had met Tom. She had brought him home with her and they had known instantly that the pair of them were in love.

The next time they had come to see Jessica's parents, it had been to announce that they were getting engaged. Lewis had asked Jessica if she had warned Tom of the problems they were going to encounter, and Lacey had secretly been amused at Jessica's insouciant, almost airy response to Lewis's question as she'd informed him that the moment she had known how she felt about Tom, which had just happened to be the day she'd met him, she had told him that she could only have female children.

'Why else do you think I want to marry her?' Tom had said with a grin later on that evening when they were all discussing the subject. 'I took one look at her mother and her sisters, and that was it. I'm going to be known as the man with those beautiful daughters, and I want at least a half a dozen of them.'

Over on the other side of the churchyard there was a small, busy flurry of activity.

'Oh, no...look at that!' Lacey protested in amusement as she watched an exasperated father rescue his small son from the lower branches of the oak tree. Not very far away her own two daughters exchanged smug smiles of female conspiracy. 'You can't let them get away with it,' Lacey told her husband. 'It's not fair that he should be punished while they put him up to it.'

'You're right. I'll go over and speak to them.'

Smiling to herself, Lacey watched him, knowing full well that retribution would be very, very slow to fall on their heads. They could both wind Lewis round their little fingers.

As she watched the page-boy being comforted by his mother she sighed a little. A boy...a son would have been nice, and perhaps for her younger daughters that might be a possibility.

Look at Michael Sullivan, for instance. He was here today, a teenager now, and, while he would never be strong, while there would always be a risk, a danger, thanks to the research the medical authorities had been able to do, the donation of bone marrow and blood cells by adult male carriers like Lewis, in Michael at least the progress of the genetic disorder had been halted.

As she watched Lewis talking to the twins, she started to walk towards them.

Lewis watched her with love in his eyes. She had given him so much and so generously. As Jessica and Tom kissed and the cameras whirred and clicked he took hold of Lacey's hand and whispered, 'Have I told you recently how much I love you?'

HARLEQUIN®
PRESENTS Plus

Meet Fin McKenzie, a woman used to dealing with all kinds of problems. Until she finds Jake Danvers asleep—and naked—in the wrong bed!

And then there's Leonie Priestley, pregnant and alone until Giles Kent, her dead fiancé's brother, tries to take control.

Fin and Leonie are just two of the passionate women you'll discover each month in Harlequin Presents Plus. And trust us, you won't want to miss meeting their men!

Watch for
PRIVATE LIVES by Carole Mortimer
Harlequin Presents Plus #1583
and
FORBIDDEN FRUIT by Charlotte Lamb
Harlequin Presents Plus #1584

Harlequin Presents Plus
The best has just gotten better!

Available in September wherever Harlequin books are sold.

Take 4 bestselling love stories FREE

Plus get a FREE surprise gift!

Special Limited-time Offer

Mail to Harlequin Reader Service®

3010 Walden Avenue
P.O. Box 1867
Buffalo, N.Y. 14269-1867

YES! Please send me 4 free Harlequin Presents® novels and my free surprise gift. Then send me 6 brand-new novels every month, which I will receive months before they appear in bookstores. Bill me at the low price of $2.24 each plus 25¢ delivery and applicable sales tax, if any*. That's the complete price and—compared to the cover prices of $2.99 each—quite a bargain! I understand that accepting the books and gift places me under no obligation ever to buy any books. I can always return a shipment and cancel at any time. Even if I never buy another book from Harlequin, the 4 free books and the surprise gift are mine to keep forever.

106 BPA AJJA

Name	(PLEASE PRINT)	
Address	Apt. No.	
City	State	Zip

This offer is limited to one order per household and not valid to present Harlequin Presents® subscribers.
*Terms and prices are subject to change without notice. Sales tax applicable in N.Y.

UPRES-93R   ©1990 Harlequin Enterprises Limited

HARLEQUIN ◆ PRESENTS®

A Year DOWN UNDER

In 1993, Harlequin Presents celebrates the land down under. In September, let us take you to Sydney, Australia, in AND THEN CAME MORNING by Daphne Clair, Harlequin Presents #1586.

Amber Wynyard's career is fulfilling—she doesn't need a man to share her life. Joel Matheson agrees...Amber doesn't need just *any* man—she needs him. But can the disturbingly unconventional Australian break down her barriers? Will Amber let Joel in on the secret she's so long concealed?

Share the adventure—and the romance—of A Year Down Under!

Available this month in
A Year Down Under

THE STONE PRINCESS
by Robyn Donald
Harlequin Presents #1577
Available wherever Harlequin books are sold.

YDU-AG

**Relive the romance...
Harlequin and Silhouette
are proud to present**

by Request™

A program of collections of three complete novels by the most
requested authors with the most requested themes. Be sure to
look for one volume each month with three complete novels by
top name authors.

In June: **NINE MONTHS** Penny Jordan
Stella Cameron
Janice Kaiser

**Three women pregnant and alone. But a lot can
happen in nine months!**

In July: **DADDY'S
HOME** Kristin James
Naomi Horton
Mary Lynn Baxter

**Daddy's Home... and his presence is long
overdue!**

In August: **FORGOTTEN
PAST** Barbara Kaye
Pamela Browning
Nancy Martin

**Do you dare to create a future if you've forgotten
the past?**

Available at your favorite retail outlet.

HARLEQUIN®   Silhouette